A MIRACLE
FOR HIS
SECRET SON

A MIRACLE
FOR HIS
SECRET SON

BY

BARBARA HANNAY

First published in Great Britain 2010
Large Print edition 2011
Harlequin Mills & Boon Limited,
Eton House, 18-24 Paradise Road,
Richmond, Surrey TW9 1SR

© Barbara Hannay 2010

ISBN: 978 0 263 22174 9

Harlequin Mills & Boon policy is to use papers that are natural, renewable and recyclable products and made from wood grown in sustainable forests. The logging and manufacturing process conform to the legal environmental regulations of the country of origin.

Printed and bound in Great Britain
by CPI Antony Rowe, Chippenham, Wiltshire

For my daughters Emma and Victoria,
always ready with bright ideas.

PROLOGUE

TELLING Gus about the baby was never going to be easy. Freya knew that.

Gus was ambitious and, in the long hours they'd spent talking about the future, he'd actually told her that he didn't want children till he was at least thirty. Just the same, all the way from Sugar Bay to Brisbane she tried to reassure herself that once she'd shared her news with Gus, he'd change his mind. How could he not want their baby? Surely everything would be fine.

Sitting on the train for five hours, nibbling dry crackers to ward off morning sickness, Freya had plenty of time to picture their reunion.

Details of the setting were hazy, but she knew exactly how Gus would look. His summer tan would have started to fade, but that was to be expected now that he was a city-based university student, attending lectures all day and poring over books at night. On the weekends too, apparently, as he'd been too busy to travel to the bay to see her.

At least his dark hair would be as soft and silky as ever, and it would still have that adorable habit of flopping forward onto his forehead. Best of all, Freya could picture the special way his dark eyes would light up when he saw her.

He would probably call her Floss, the funny nickname he'd given her within days of his arrival at Sugar Bay High. He'd look at her with one of his heartbreakingly beautiful smiles and he'd gather her in so close she could feel his heart pumping. She'd breathe in the scent of his skin, and her off-kilter world would settle back into place.

Later, when they were quite alone, she would find the courage to tell him.

Then, it would be OK.

She was silly to worry. Once Gus got used to the idea of the baby, they would work out *something* together and her future would no longer be a scary black hole. She would have Gus and their baby. Everything would be fine.

Deep in her heart, Freya knew that she might be nervous now, but by the end of the day, she and Gus would have a plan. Really, there was no need to worry.

CHAPTER ONE

LATE on a Friday afternoon, Gus Wilder was only half paying attention when he lifted the receiver.

'A long-distance call for you, boss,' Charlie from the front office told him. 'A Freya Jones from Sugar Bay in Queensland.'

Freya Jones.

Just like that, Gus was zapped from his demountable office in the remotest corner of the Northern Territory to a little beach town on the coast of Queensland. He was eighteen again and standing at the edge of rolling surf, gazing into a lovely girl's laughing sea-green eyes.

It was twelve years since he'd left the Bay and he hadn't seen Freya in all that time, but of course he remembered her. Perfectly.

Didn't every man remember the sweet, fragile magic of his first love?

So much water had flowed under the bridge

since then. He'd finished his studies and worked in foreign continents, and he'd traversed joyous and difficult journeys of the heart. Freya would have changed a lot too. No doubt she was married. Some lucky guy was sure to have snapped her up by now.

He couldn't think why she would be ringing him after all this time. Was there a high school reunion? Bad news about an old schoolmate?

Charlie spoke again. 'Boss, you going to take the call?'

'Yes, sure.' Gus swallowed to ease the unexpected tension in his throat. 'Put Freya on.'

He heard her voice. 'Gus?'

Amazing. She could still infuse a single syllable with music. Her voice had always been like that—light, lyrical and sensuous.

'Hello, Freya.'

'You must be surprised to hear from me. Quite a blast from the past.'

Now she sounded nervous, totally unlike the laughing, confident girl Gus remembered. A thousand questions clamoured to be asked, but instinctively, he skipped the usual *how are you?* preliminaries… 'How can I help you, Freya?'

There was an almost inaudible sigh. 'I'm afraid it's really hard to explain over the phone. But it's important, Gus. Really important. I…I was hoping I could meet with you.'

Stunned, he took too long to respond. 'Sure,' he said at last. 'But I'm tied up right now. When do you want to meet?'

'As soon as possible?'

This obviously wasn't about a high school reunion. Gus shot a quick glance through the window of his makeshift office to the untamed bushland that stretched endlessly to ancient red cliffs on the distant horizon. 'You know I'm way up in Arnhem Land, don't you?'

'Yes, they told me you're managing a remote housing project for an Aboriginal community.'

'That's right.' The project was important and challenging, requiring a great deal of diplomacy from Gus as its manager. 'It's almost impossible for me to get away from here just now. What's this all about?'

'I could come to you.'

Gus swallowed his shock. Why would Freya come to him here? After all this time? What on earth could be so suddenly important?

His mind raced, trying to dredge up possibilities, but each time he drew a blank.

He pictured Freya as he remembered her, with long sun-streaked hair and golden tanned limbs, more often than not in a bikini with a faded sarong loosely tied around her graceful hips. Even if she'd cast aside her sea nymph persona, she was bound to cause an impossible stir if she arrived on the all-male construction site.

'It would be too difficult here,' he said. 'This place is too...remote.'

'Don't planes fly into your site?'

'We don't have regular commercial flights.'

'Oh.'

Another eloquent syllable—and there was no mistaking her disappointment.

Grimacing, Gus scratched at his jaw. 'You said this was very important.'

'Yes, it is.' After a beat, Freya said in a small frightened voice, 'It's a matter of life and death.'

They agreed to meet in Darwin, the Northern Territory's capital, which was, in many ways, an idyllic spot for a reunion, especially at sunset on a Saturday evening at the end of a balmy tropical winter. The sky above the harbour glowed bright blushing pink shot with gold. The palm trees were graceful dancing silhouettes on the shorefront and the colours of the sky were reflected in the still tropical waters.

Not that Freya could appreciate the view.

She arrived too early on the hotel balcony. It wasn't very crowded and she saw immediately that Gus wasn't there, so she sat at the nearest free table, with her legs crossed and one foot swinging impatiently, while her fingers anxiously twisted the straps of her shoulder bag.

These nervous habits were new to her and she hated them. Having grown up in a free and easy beachside community, she'd prided herself on her relaxed personality and as an adult she'd added meditation and yoga to her daily practice.

Her serenity had deserted her, however, on the day she'd needed it most—when the doctor delivered his prognosis. Since then she'd been living with sickening fear, barely holding herself together with a string and a paper clip.

Freya closed her eyes and took a deep breath, then concentrated on imagining her son at home with Poppy, her mother. If Nick wasn't taking his dog, Urchin, for a twilight run on the beach, he'd be sprawled on the living room carpet, playing with his solar-powered robot grasshopper. Poppy would be preparing dinner in the nearby kitchen, slipping in as many healthy vegetables as she dared.

Already Freya missed her boy. She'd never been so far away from him before and, thinking of him now, and the task that lay ahead of her, she felt distinctly weepy. She dashed tears away with the heel of her hand. Heavens, she couldn't weaken now. She had to stay super-strong.

You can do this. You must do this. For Nick.

She'd do anything for Nick, even tell Gus Wilder the truth after all this time.

That thought caused another explosion of fear. The process of tracking Gus down and making the first telephone contact had been the easy part. The worst was yet to come. Gus still didn't know why she needed him.

A tall, flashily handsome waiter passed Freya, carrying a tray laden with drinks. The smile he gave her was flirtatious to the point of predation. 'Would you like something from the bar, madam?'

'Not just now, thanks. I'm waiting for...' The rest of Freya's sentence died as her throat closed over.

Beyond the waiter, she saw a man coming through the wide open doorway onto the balcony.

Gus.

Tall. Dark-haired. White shirt gleaming against tanned skin. Perhaps a little leaner than she remembered, but handsome and athletic enough to make heads turn.

Angus Wilder had aged very nicely, thank you.

But what kind of man was he now? How many gulfs had widened between them, and how would he react to her news?

As he made his way towards her, weaving between tables, memories, like scenes in a movie, played in Freya's head. Gus at sixteen on his first day at Sugar Bay High, desperate to throw off the taint of his posh city high school. Gus, triumphant on the footie field after he'd scored a match-winning try. Herself, floating with happiness as she danced in his arms at the senior formal.

The two of them walking together, holding hands beside a moonlit sea. The sheer romance of their first kiss...

Suddenly Gus was beside her, leaning down to drop a polite kiss on her cheek. 'Freya, it's good to see you.'

He smelled clean, as if he'd just showered and splashed on aftershave. His lips were warm on her skin.

Without warning, Freya's eyes and throat stung. 'It's great to see *you*, Gus.' She blinked hard. This was no time for nostalgia. She had to stay cool and focused. 'Thanks for coming.'

He pulled out a chair and sat, then slowly crossed his long legs and leaned back, as if he were deliberately trying to appear relaxed. His smile was cautious, the expression in his dark eyes warm, but puzzled. 'How are you?' Quickly, he countered his question. 'You look fabulous.'

Deep down she couldn't help being pleased by the compliment, but she said simply, 'I'm well, thanks. How about you? How's business?'

'Both first-rate.' Gus sent her a slightly less careful smile, but his throat worked, betraying his tension. 'So, I take it you still live at the Bay?'

'I do.' She smiled shyly and gave a careless flick of her long pale hair. 'Still a beach girl.'

'It suits you.'

Freya dampened her lips and prepared to launch into what had to be said.

'How's your mother?' Gus asked, jumping in to fill the brief lull.

'Oh, she's fine, thanks. Still living in the same crooked little house right on the beachfront. As much of a hippie as ever.'

He let his gaze travel over her and, despite the nervous knots tightening in her stomach, Freya indulged in a little staring too. His eyes were as rich and dark as ever and his hair still had the habit of flopping forward onto his forehead.

She felt an ache in her chest—she couldn't help it. She'd missed Gus Wilder so much. For a dozen years she'd been out of his life. She knew he'd worked in Africa, and there was so much more she wanted to know. Where exactly had he been? What had he done and seen? Whom had he loved?

'I know you have something very important to discuss,' Gus said, 'but would you like a drink first?' Without waiting for her answer, he raised a hand to catch the waiter's attention.

'What can I get for you?' The waiter's manner was noticeably less cordial now that Gus had joined Freya.

'A lemon, lime and bitters, please,' she said.

'And I'll have a mid-strength beer.'

'Very well, sir.'

After he'd gone, another awkward silence fell and Freya knew it was up to her to speak. If she didn't get to the point of this meeting quickly it would become impossibly difficult. Taking a deep breath, she folded her hands carefully in her lap.

'I really am very grateful that you've come here, Gus. I know you must be puzzled, but I'm hoping that you might be able to help me.'

'You said it was a matter of life and death.'

She nodded.

'I hoped you were being melodramatic.'

'Unfortunately, no.'

The last remnants of Gus's smile vanished. Leaning forward, he reached for her hand. 'Freya, what is it? What's happened?'

His touch was so gentle and he looked so

worried she had to close her eyes. She hadn't been able to broach this subject twelve years ago, and it was a thousand times harder now. Just thinking about what she had to tell him made her heart race and her stomach rebel.

'Gus, before I tell you, I have to ask—are you married?'

It was the worst possible moment for the waiter to return. Wincing, Freya dropped her gaze while the drinks were set on cardboard coasters in front of them.

She reached for her purse, but Gus beat her to the draw.

'My shout,' he said.

'But I owc you. You'vc comc all this way.'

He was already handing money to the waiter and she didn't feel strong enough to argue. Instead, she thanked him and stirred her drink with a slim black straw, making the ice cubes clink and the slices of lemon and lime swirl.

Frowning, Gus touched the tips of two fingers to the frosty outside of his beer glass. 'I can't help being curious. What does my marital status have to do with your problem?'

She felt her cheeks grow hot. 'It…could…

complicate everything. If you were married, your wife might not want you to help me.'

Heavens, she was making a mess of this and Gus looked understandably puzzled. She wished she could find a way to simply download everything she needed to tell him without stumbling through explanations, or grasping for the right words, or the right order to put them in. Surely, negotiating world peace would be easier than this.

Clearly bewildered, Gus shot a glance to her left hand. 'What about you? Are you married?'

'Still single.'

His eyes widened. 'That's a surprise. I thought you'd be snapped up by now.'

I never gave them a chance, Freya thought.

Gus set his glass down and eyed her levelly. 'I *was* married three years ago,' he said.

She had steeled herself, determined not to mind, but this wasn't just a matter of hurt pride. She did mind. Very much. Now Gus would have to discuss her problem with his wife and how could she be sure another woman would be sympathetic?

Gus swallowed, making the muscles in his throat ripple. 'My wife died.'

'Oh.' A whisper was all Freya could manage. She was swamped by a deluge of emotions—sympathy and sadness for Gus mixed, heaven help her, with jealousy for the woman who'd won his heart. 'Gus, I'm so sorry. Were you married long?'

'A little over a year. We met when we were both working in Africa. My wife, Monique, was French—a doctor with Médecins Sans Frontières.'

So his wife had been clever, adventurous and courageous, and filled with high ideals. In other words, she was exactly like Gus. She'd been perfect for him.

'That's so sad.' To her shame, Freya was torn between compassion for Gus's pain and her relief that one hurdle had been removed.

Gus said grimly, 'I guess you'd better tell me what this is all about. What's your problem?'

Her heart took off like a steeplechaser. 'Actually, it's my son who's in trouble.'

'Your *son*?' Gus repeated, clearly shocked.

All the worry and tension of the past weeks rose inside Freya and she felt like a pressure cooker about to blow its lid. Her lips trembled, but she willed herself to hold everything together. She mustn't break down now.

'So you're a single mum?'

She nodded, too choked up to speak.

'Like your mother.'

She managed another nod, grateful for the lack of condemnation in his voice. Of course, Gus had never been a snob like his father. He'd never looked down his nose at Sugar Bay's hippies.

Just the same, his observation was accurate. Freya had followed in her mother's footsteps. In fact, Poppy had actively encouraged her daughter into single motherhood.

We can raise your baby together, darling. Of course we can. Look at the way I raised you. We'll be fine. We're alike, you and me. We're destined to be independent. You don't need a man, love.

Unfortunately, Poppy had been wrong. The terrible day had arrived when neither of them was able to help Nick—and Freya had no choice but to seek help from this man, his father.

Gus was watching her closely, his expression a mixture of frowning puzzlement and tender concern. 'Are you still in contact with the boy's father?'

It was too much. Her eyes filled with tears. She'd waited too long to tell him this—twelve years too long—and now she had to deliver a terrible blow. It was so, *so* difficult. She didn't want to hurt him.

She had no choice.

Clinging to the last shreds of composure, she looked away from him to the flat sea stained with the spectacular colours of the sunset. She blinked hard and her throat felt as if she'd swallowed broken glass.

Beside them, a party of young people arrived on the balcony, laughing and carefree, carrying their drinks and calling to each other as they dragged tables together and sat in a large happy circle. It was a scenario Freya had seen many, many times at the pub on the Sugar Bay waterfront. Once, she and Gus had been part of a crowd just like that.

Terrified that she might cry in public and cause Gus all kinds of embarrassment, she said, 'I'm sorry. Would you mind if we went somewhere else to talk about this? We could go for a walk, perhaps?'

'Of course.'

Gallantly, he rose immediately and they took the short flight of steps down to The Esplanade that skirted Darwin Harbour.

Offshore, yachts were racing, bright spinnakers billowing, leaning into a light breeze. The same breeze brought the salty-sharp smell of coral mingled with the scent of frangipani blossoms. The breeze played with Freya's hair and she didn't try to hold it in place. Instead, she wrapped her arms protectively over her front as Gus walked beside her, his hands sunk in the pockets of his light-coloured chinos.

'Are you OK, Freya?'

'Sort of.' She took a deep breath, knowing that she couldn't put this revelation off a second longer. 'You asked if I've been in touch with my son's father.'

'Yes.'

'I haven't, Gus.'

She slid a wary sideways glance his way and she saw the exact moment when he realised. Saw his eyes widen with dawning knowledge, and then a flash of horror.

He stopped walking.

The colour drained from his face as he stared at her. 'How old is this boy?'

His voice was cold and quiet, and Freya's heart pounded so loudly it drummed in her ears.

'He's eleven—almost eleven and a half.'

Gus shook his head. 'No way.'

He glared at her, his eyes angry—disbelieving—already rejecting what she had to tell him next.

CHAPTER TWO

Gus struggled to breathe, struggled to think, to believe, to understand…but, all the while, gut-level awareness was shouting the truth that Freya still hadn't told him.

He had a son. A boy. Now eleven years old.

'Gus, I'm so sorry.' Freya stood on the path in front of him, wringing her hands, her face a blurred wash of tears.

His mind flashed back to their past, to the last magical summer he'd spent at the Bay—three halcyon months between the end of high school and the start of university—when he and Freya had been almost inseparable.

Twelve years had passed since then and in many ways it had felt like a lifetime. Now, for Gus, it felt like a lifetime in exile.

He rounded on her. 'Say it, Freya. Spit it out. This boy is my son, isn't he?'

Shoulders back, chin lifted, she met his angry gaze. 'Yes, Gus, you're Nick's father.'

'Nick?'

'He's Nicholas Angus.'

A terrible ache bloomed in his throat, swiftly followed by a tumult of emotions—alienation and loneliness, frustration and anger. He spun away from her, fighting for composure. The sea breeze buffeted his face and he gulped in deep needy breaths.

He tried to picture his son, this boy he'd never seen. His flesh and blood. Damn it, he had no idea what the kid might look like.

How crazy was that?

His thoughts flew haphazardly. He had a son. Every boy needed a dad. What right had Freya to keep such a secret?

Had it worked both ways? Did the boy know anything about him?

Unlikely.

Gus whirled back to challenge Freya. 'Why? Why the hell didn't you tell me?' He knew he sounded bitter but he didn't care. He *was* bitter. 'Did you keep this to yourself because you didn't know who *your* father was? Is it some kind of warped tradition in your family?'

'No, of course not.'

Her protest wasn't convincing but he didn't stop to investigate. 'Why then? Why didn't you tell me that I had a son?'

'I thought—' Freya's hands flailed with a wild kind of helplessness, then fell to her sides and she gave a groan of frustration. 'I tried, Gus. I did try to tell you.'

'When?' he shouted, not trying to hide his disbelief.

'The day I came to the university to see you.'

His mouth sagged open as memories of that day arrived in a sickening rush. His skin flashed hot and cold and a feeling suspiciously like guilt curdled unpleasantly in his stomach.

Over the years, he'd blotted out Freya's sudden appearance on the St Lucia campus, but he couldn't deny that he'd never felt comfortable about the last time they'd met.

Now, she was walking away from him, leaving the walking track and hurrying across the velvety lawn to the rocks that bordered the foreshore. By the time Gus reached her, she'd pulled tissues from a woven shoulder bag and was blowing her nose.

'We have to talk about this,' he said.

'Of course. That's why we're here.' She spoke with quiet resignation.

They found a flat rock to sit on—side by side, looking out to sea—and it was uncannily like old times, except that, unlike the pounding surf in Sugar Bay, this sea was flat and calm. And they were facing west now, rather than east, so the setting sun was suspended inches above the horizon like a giant glowing balloon.

Freya shoved the tissues back into her bag, then drew an elaborately deep breath and let it out very slowly.

Despite his rage and frustration, Gus couldn't help thinking how lovely she looked, sitting on the rock beside the sea.

She directed her steady gaze his way, giving him the full effect of her darkly lashed aquamarine eyes. 'Do you remember that day I came to see you at university?'

'Of course.'

'I was, honestly, planning to tell you that I was pregnant.'

'But you didn't say a thing about it. Not a word.' He fought to speak calmly. 'Why?'

She dropped her gaze. 'It's hard to explain now, after such a long time. I know I was very young and immature back then. I was totally freaked by the whole university scene.'

The wind plucked at her hair and she caught a strand and tucked it behind her ear. To his dismay, Gus found himself noticing the delicate shape of her ear and the small hole pierced in the middle of her neat pale lobe.

'The whole journey to Brisbane was such a big deal for me,' she said. 'I had to travel such a long way from the Bay on the train, and I had to get up at something like four o'clock in the morning. And I had morning sickness, so I was pretty fragile. Then, when I got to Brisbane, I had to catch the bus out to St Lucia. When I arrived there, and the university was so—'

She waved her hands, searching for the word.

'Intimidating?'

'Yes. So huge and important-looking. All those sandstone buildings and columns and courtyards.'

Gus nodded. It was incredibly easy, now, to

imagine how a girl from a sleepy beach village had felt, but he'd been young, too. Looking back, he suspected that he had, quite possibly, been insensitive.

Freya pouted. 'I'd told you I was coming, so I thought you'd skip a lecture to see me. But I had to wait around for ages for you to come out of the lecture hall and then, when you did, you were surrounded by a tribe of adoring women.'

Gus felt his neck redden as he remembered. 'Hardly a tribe. And there were other guys in the group.'

She dismissed this with a sharp laugh. 'I was naïve, I guess, but I got such a shock to see how you'd changed so quickly. After all, it was only about six weeks since I'd seen you.'

'I couldn't have been too different, surely?'

She lifted her hands, palms up. 'Believe me, Gus, you were different in every way. You had this scholarly air. And you were so full of how awesome university was. You couldn't stop talking about your college and your lecturers, your career plans. After six weeks at uni, you were going to single-handedly save the Third World.'

Gus swallowed uncomfortably, knowing she was right.

'And those girls were such snobs,' Freya said. 'Designer jeans, masses of jewellery, perfect hair and make-up. I hated the way they looked down their noses at me.'

'I'm sure they didn't.'

Freya rolled her eyes as if he hadn't a clue. 'They made it clear that I had no right to be there, chasing after you.'

Gus remembered how Freya had looked that day, dressed in her hippie, beach girl get-up like something out of the seventies, in a batik wrap-around skirt, a silver anklet complete with bells and brown leather sandals.

He'd thought she'd looked fine. She was Freya, after all. But he could guess how those city girls might have made her feel. No doubt they'd used that particularly sinister feminine radar that sent out signals undetected by males.

Why hadn't he been more perceptive? More protective of his girlfriend?

Even to him, it no longer made sense.

But *hang on*. He might not have shown

exemplary sensitivity, but Freya still should have told him she was pregnant.

Gus turned to her. 'How could you have been pregnant? We took precautions.'

She lifted an eyebrow and the look she sent him was decidedly arch. 'If you remember, you weren't exactly an expert at using a condom.'

He groaned, muttered "Idiot" under his breath.

Face aflame, he looked out to sea where the last of the sun's crimson light was melting into the darkening water. 'If you'd told me, Freya, if you'd given me a chance, I would have faced up to my responsibilities.'

'I suppose you would have.' Her fingers began to twist the woven straps of her shoulder bag. 'But you'd told me you didn't want children for ages.'

'That didn't mean—' Gus grimaced and shook his head.

'I didn't want you to see me as a responsibility. I wanted to be so much more to you, Gus, but when I saw you that day I lost all my confidence. I knew what becoming a father would have cost you. Your father had such high hopes for you.

And you had big dreams too. A baby would have wrecked everything you had planned.'

'I'd have found a way.'

Her steady gaze challenged him. 'Be honest. Your father organised a transfer back to Brisbane, just so he and your mother could support you through uni. You were their eldest son, the jewel in their crowns. They'd never have forgiven you. And how would you have felt if you'd had to leave your studies to earn enough money to maintain a family?'

'I don't know,' Gus said glumly. 'I wasn't given the opportunity to find out.'

It was ages before Freya said softly, 'Well, OK, I think we've established that I made a bad call.' She dropped her gaze, but not before he saw the glitter of tears in her eyes. 'I've said I'm sorry. But sometimes mistakes are made with the best of intentions.'

Gus let out a heavy sigh and wondered to what degree his overbearing parents had swayed Freya's decision. The irony was that as soon as he'd graduated he hadn't gone into the kind of high profile executive position his father had planned for him. He'd quietly rebelled and gone off to Africa instead. Bursting with high ideals, he'd dived into aid work.

For the next nine years he'd been committed to doing good work for strangers and, sure, they'd really needed help. But, all that time, there'd been a son who'd needed him back in Australia.

The thought of that boy made him want to cry out with rage. Despair. Self-pity. Where was the morality in trying to save the world when he'd contributed absolutely zilch to his own son's welfare?

The worst of it was that Freya *had* tried to tell him.

She'd turned to him in trouble and, instead of becoming the prince who rescued her, he'd let her down. Very badly, it seemed.

Oh, he'd gone through the motions that day. Resisting the crass option to sneak her back to his college room for a quick tumble between the sheets, he'd taken Freya back into the city on the bus and splashed out on an expensive supper at a posh café overlooking the Brisbane River. But throughout the meal she'd been strained.

Looking back, he could see that he'd been far too impressed with himself as a student. Too caught up in his new and exciting world. He probably hadn't given Freya a chance to get a word in edgeways.

Guiltily, he remembered that he'd been rather relieved to put her back on the train to Sugar Bay. It was only when he'd walked along the railway platform, keeping up with her carriage as the train lumbered off, that he'd seen the tears streaming down her face.

Too late, he'd understood that he'd disappointed her. And now, *way* too late, he realised that he'd been so self-absorbed he'd left no room for her to offload her dilemma. He'd been a complete ass.

The big question was—if he *had* known about the baby, would he have made room in his life for Freya? Happily? Without resentment?

He'd loved her, sure. That summer with her was his sweetest, most poignant memory. But, in that first term at university, he'd loved the idea of Freya waiting back in Sugar Bay far more than the reality of her intruding into his busy new life.

Gus sat in silence, mustering his thoughts while he listened to the soft lapping of the sea. After a bit, he said, 'You stopped answering my letters.'

'We decided it was better to make a clean break.'

'We?' For a moment he imagined she was talking about another boyfriend. Then he remembered Poppy. Freya's mother had always been more like her sister or her best friend than her mother. 'I suppose Poppy was in on this too. She very effectively blocked my phone calls.'

'She was a tower of strength.'

Oh, yeah, she would have been, Gus thought grimly. Poppy would have been in her element. She'd never been able to hang on to a man for long, but she would have clung for dear life to Freya and the promise of a grandchild. She would have aided and abetted Freya's decision to end it with him and raise the baby alone.

So it boiled down to the fact that his relationship with Freya had just faded away. She hadn't answered him and he, distracted by his bright new world, had simply let her go.

In other words, he, Freya and Poppy had made separate choices twelve years ago, and now they were paying the price.

Rather, the boy, Nick, was paying the price.

Gus looked up at the darkening sky—navy-blue,

almost black—and he saw the evening star, already shining and sitting alone in the heavens like a bright solitaire diamond.

Staring at it, he felt shock like a fist slamming into his solar plexus. *Hell.* He still didn't know why Freya had contacted him so urgently. He'd been hung up about what happened in the past, but hadn't she said that her son had a problem right here and now?

A matter of life and death?

He bit back a horrified groan. 'There's more, isn't there? You still haven't told me why you need my help.'

To Gus's dismay, Freya seemed to slump beside him as if her strength had suddenly deserted her. He reached out, wanting to draw her against him, to rest her head against his shoulder, but his hand hovered inches from her. 'What is it? What's happened?'

A sob tore from her throat and she covered her face with her hands.

A hot knife of fear sliced through Gus. For an instant he felt an urge to flee, to refuse to listen to her bad news. He couldn't bear the tension.

He forced himself to speak. 'Is...is the boy sick?'

Freya nodded and the knife in his guts twisted sharper, deeper. *Life and death*. Terror chilled his blood. Was his son dying?

His throat tightened painfully. He hadn't known it was possible to care so instantly and painfully for a boy he'd never met.

Freya, sensing Gus's distress, lifted her head. Hands clenched in her lap, she sat very still, willing herself to be strong. This was the point of no return, the worst part of her mission. She couldn't fail her boy now.

So many times she'd thought about what she would say to Gus at this moment, and she'd searched for the wisest and kindest starting point. Each time she'd come up with one answer. She had to tell him the hard news straight up.

This wasn't a time for breaking things gently. To pussyfoot around would be both cruel and unhelpful.

But...oh, God. She felt as if she were plunging from the highest possible diving board into the tiniest thimble of safety.

She thought of Nick again—her gorgeous,

talented rascal of a boy—and she knew she had no choice. Taking a deep breath, she said, quietly but clearly, so there could be no mistake. 'Nick's kidneys are failing and he needs a transplant.'

It was almost dark but Freya didn't miss Gus's reaction. It was like watching a man in agony turn to stone.

Horrified, she began to shake and she closed her eyes, unable to bear the sight of his distress. *I'm sorry, Gus. I wouldn't have done this to you if I'd had a choice. But I had no choice. I'm so, so sorry.*

The awful silence seemed to stretch for ever. Somewhere overhead fruit bats screeched and chased each other, tattered black wings flapping noisily as they raced on their nightly raid of local gardens.

It was a full minute before Gus spoke and, when he did, his voice was dull and lifeless, dropping into the tropical night like a handful of pebbles thudding onto sand.

'I guess you're on the hunt for a donor. That's why you need me.'

Freya tried to answer but when she opened her

mouth a noisy sob broke from her. Blindly, she groped in her bag for her tissues.

'I'm so sorry,' she spluttered. 'I know this is the worst possible way to find out.'

'You're not wrong.' His tone was disturbingly unreadable.

She bit down on her bottom lip to stifle another sob. She couldn't imagine how Gus felt, but she knew it would be beyond heartbreaking to be told one minute that he had an eleven-year-old son and then... *Oh, by the way, we're hoping you can give the boy your kidney.*

Gus couldn't help but be shocked and angry but, when he spoke, his tone was almost expressionless. 'I assume you're not a suitable donor.'

Freya shook her head. 'Poppy and I both wanted to help, but we're the wrong blood type.' The breeze blowing across the water turned chilly and she shivered.

'We're both type B and Nick is O, so we knew that you must be O as well. Apparently, type B people can receive type O kidneys, but people who have O blood can only receive a kidney from another type O donor.'

Beside her, Gus was moving, lurching to his

feet. In a heartbeat he'd shifted from the rock onto the grass. When Freya tried to follow, he held up his hands, warning her to stay put.

'Give me a moment,' he said stiffly. 'I just need to…to get my head around this.'

'Of course.'

He began to pace back and forth, jaw tight, hands thrust deep in his pockets, his dark hair lifted by the wind. Abruptly, he stopped pacing and stood glaring out to sea.

Freya opened her mouth to say something— anything that might serve as a peace offering— but she had no idea what to say. She knew Gus was battling a storm of emotions and he needed space. Head space. Emotional space.

She could only pray that, somewhere within that turmoil, he could find it in his heart to help Nick.

Suddenly, he whirled on her, his face pale, eyes wild, arms stiff by his sides, fists clenched.

'Gus,' she said hesitantly, 'are you OK?'

Oh, God, what a stupid, *stupid* question.

His cold laugh mocked her. 'You've got to be joking.' He prowled closer, his body taut as a hunter's, his expression dark and menacing. 'Of course I'm not OK. I'm mad, Freya. I'm mad with you. With Poppy. With a crazy universe that lets this happen to *my* kid. To anybody's kid.'

She hadn't moved from the rock but she realised now that she'd drawn her knees up and wrapped her arms around them, turning her body into a defensive ball.

She'd never seen Gus like this. 'I don't blame you for being mad with me.'

'Hell. If this hadn't happened, you'd never have told me about the boy, would you? You only made contact with me now as a last resort.'

What could Freya say? It was the awful truth. Things might have been different if Gus hadn't been away in the depths of Africa for nine years…or if her own father hadn't turned up, out of the blue, proving that family reunions could be disastrous…

'Damn it, Freya, if you or Poppy had been able to help Nick, you'd have let me go my entire life-time without ever knowing my son existed.'

She shook her head, but Gus had already spun away again. He'd had too many shocks at once and he was hurt, deeply hurt.

She wished she hadn't had to do this to him.

Wished she'd made wiser choices earlier. But, even if she had been braver, even if everything had turned out miraculously and she and Gus had been married and raised Nick in a perfect fairy tale family, she couldn't have stopped Nick getting sick.

Gus still would have faced this challenge.

But of course he had every right to be angry. She half-expected him to grab a rock and hurl it into the sea.

Instead, he slammed a balled fist into his palm, then stood, hands on hips, breathing deeply, dragging in lungfuls of fresh sea air.

Watching him, Freya felt a band of pain encircle her heart, squeezing painfully. Her vision blurred.

She reached for the tissues again. She'd been tense for weeks and now she felt stretched to breaking point. She still didn't know if Gus would help her.

Was she asking too much of him?

Poor man. He'd had such a lot to deal with—the death of his wife and the demands of Africa and, more recently, managing big remote area projects. And they were just the few things she knew about—heaven knew what else he had on his plate. And now, her news about Nick must have hit him like a bombshell exploding in his face.

She remembered how she'd felt a couple of months ago on the day the doctor had given her the bad news. Heartsick and desperate, she'd paced along the beach and she'd soon found that she couldn't stop. She'd forgotten to take a hat but she didn't care. She'd walked the entire length of Sugar Bay and then she'd climbed over the headland and onto the next bay and the bay after that.

She'd come home sunburnt and exhausted but she still hadn't been able to sleep that night. Actually, she hadn't slept properly since that day, and even when she had slept she'd either had nightmares about losing Nick or dreams in which Nick was cured and well, only to wake to cruel reality. She'd lived with gnawing fear as her constant companion.

Now, Gus was turning back to her once more, his expression grave yet purposeful. Freya wondered if this meant he'd reached a decision and nervous chills chased each other down her arms.

Her stomach bunched into terrified knots but she forced her facial muscles to relax. She didn't want to let Gus see how frightened she was.

As he approached her, she scrambled stiffly to her feet and, to her surprise, he held out his hand to help her down from the rock.

Freya held her breath.

'Relax, Freya. I'm more than willing to help Nick, if I can.'

A massive wave of relief washed over her.

She knew that at some point in the very near future she'd be ecstatic and dancing with gratitude, but right now she couldn't manage words of more than one syllable. 'Thanks.'

'Hey, you're shaking,' Gus said.

He was still holding her hand and, for a moment, she thought he was going to put his arms around her. Her mind took a ridiculous leap, instantly imagining his embrace and her head cradled against his broad shoulder.

Oh, heavens, how she longed to be there, in the protective shelter of Gus Wilder's arms, whispering her thanks while she drew strength and comfort from him. She could almost imagine the remembered scent of his skin mingled with the fragrance of the tropical night.

But of course Gus had no intention of hugging her. How silly to have even thought of it. She'd surrendered that privilege a very long time ago.

'You're cold,' he said. 'Your fingers are practically frozen.' In a purely practical gesture, he rubbed her fingers between his warm palms and she loved it, even though she shouldn't. 'You should go inside, Freya. You're dressed for summer.'

'I didn't think it ever got cold in Darwin.'

'Sure it does. Every year there are at least three days when Darwinians have to put their jackets on.'

He'd almost cracked a joke. Surely that was a good sign.

Gus let her hand go and they walked side by side across the grass to the well-lit concrete path that led back to the hotel.

'So,' he said briskly, 'I guess you'd better tell me what you know about Nick's condition. I'd like to be fully in the picture.'

He deserved no less, and she'd almost learned to talk about Nick's illness dispassionately, the way the doctors did, hiding the personal terror that lurked behind every word.

'It started with a bad case of stomach flu. Vomiting and a high fever. I realised Nick was getting dehydrated, so I took him to the doctor, to our local GP. He took one look at him and rushed him to hospital, to emergency.'

She couldn't help shuddering, reliving the horror. 'Nick seemed to make a good recovery from that, but there were follow-up blood tests, and that's when possible problems showed up.' A sigh escaped her. 'So we were sent to Brisbane then, to see a specialist, and they discovered that Nick had a disease called global glomerulosclerosis.'

'That's a mouthful.'

'Yes. I'm afraid I've had plenty of practice at saying it. Nick calls it his global warning.'

'What a champ.' Gus's smile was tinged with sadness. 'It takes courage to make a joke about something so personally threatening.'

'He's been incredibly brave.' Freya blinked back tears. 'I've been a mess. So scared. I used to burst into tears without warning. Day and night. But then I saw how strong Nick was and I realised I had to toughen up for his sake.'

Gus remembered young mothers in Africa, broken-hearted, watching their children grow weaker while they covered their fear behind a mask of stoicism. He hated to think of Freya bearing the same kind of pain for her son—*their* son.

'Basically,' Freya continued, 'this disease means that Nick's kidneys are filling up with scar tissue. Eventually it leads to complete kidney failure.'

She stopped walking. They were almost back at the hotel and the carefree sounds of laughter and music from a jukebox spilled into the night.

'He's been on medication for the past couple of months,' she said. 'And it's working really well. He feels fine but, unfortunately, the medication will only work for a limited time.' She looked up and met Gus's stern gaze. 'That's why he needs a transplant.'

'Poor kid.' Gus's throat worked furiously. 'Does he understand?'

Freya nodded and, despite her tension, she smiled. 'On the surface, he doesn't seem too worried. He feels fine and he doesn't need dialysis. That's a huge plus. The drugs have allowed him to carry on as usual. He can still swim and play sport, take his dog for a run.'

'He has a dog?'

'Yes. An ugly little mix of terrier and heaven knows what from the Animal Shelter. Nick adores him. Calls him Urchin. They share every spare minute Nick isn't at school. They're the best of mates.'

Gus's eyes took on a misty faraway look and Freya was almost certain that he was picturing the boy and the dog, running on the beach at Sugar Bay. The fond warmth in his eyes made her throat ache.

Next moment, Gus blinked and the soft light was gone. His expression was sober again. 'So he understands about needing a transplant?'

'Yes.' She gave an imitation of Nick's typical shrug. 'But he doesn't dwell on it.'

'The benefits of being young, I guess.' Gus dropped his gaze and sighed.

'We don't talk about the alternative,' she said softly. 'I've promised him I'll find a donor.'

'Have you tried elsewhere?'

Freya looked away. 'We're on a waiting list, but the doctor said that you were our best chance, Gus.'

He nodded grimly. 'And the time frame?'

'The sooner he has the transplant, the better.'

'Let's hope I can help then.'

'It would be—' Freya's mouth trembled. She wanted to shower Gus with gratitude. This was such a huge thing he was offering—to submit to an operation, to hand over a vital organ.

But her instincts told her that he wouldn't welcome such effusiveness from her. He was still shocked and angry. Just the same, she had to say something. 'I…I'm so sorry to land this on you. I know it's a terrible shock and a huge imposition, and I—'

He held up a hand, silencing her. 'It's not an imposition.' Harsh anger simmered beneath the quiet surface of his voice. 'I'm the boy's father.'

Chastened, Freya nodded. Gus's reaction was just as she'd expected. He was prepared to help his son, and that was the best she could hope for. It would be too much to expect him to forgive her secrecy.

'You never know,' Gus said less harshly. 'This might be Nick's lucky day.'

To her surprise, he smiled. Admittedly, it was a crooked, rather sad smile, but it encouraged an answering smile from her. 'I certainly hope so.'

'But it's not just a matter of matching blood types, is it?'

'Blood type is the major hurdle, but there are other tests they need to do. I know there's a chest X-ray, but I'm not totally sure about everything else. I was ruled unsuitable before I got past first base.'

It was then Freya realised that she'd been so stressed and worried about Nick that she hadn't actually planned anything for this meeting beyond asking Gus for his help. Now, she wondered if she should ask him to join her for dinner. 'Are you staying in this hotel?'

'Yes.'

Unexpected heat flamed in her cheeks. 'Do you have plans for this evening?'

'Nothing special beyond meeting you.'

'I wasn't sure…if you'd…like to have dinner.'

Looking mildly surprised, he said dryly, 'I certainly need to eat.'

Had he deliberately missed her point? Freya felt confused but she also felt compelled to hold out an olive branch. She was so enormously indebted to him, and so very much in the wrong.

Running her tongue over parched lips, she tried

again. 'Please, let me take you to dinner. After all, it's the least I can do.'

His wary eyes narrowed ever so slightly and she held her breath, knowing she would enjoy dining with him very much. There was so much to talk about, and they could possibly begin to build bridges.

'Thank you, but not tonight,' Gus said quietly and he reached into his shirt pocket and pulled out his door key, checking its number. 'I'm in Room 607,' he said. 'Perhaps you could ring me in the morning to give me the doctors' contact details.'

'Yes, sure.'

'For now I'll say goodnight, then.'

Freya swallowed her disappointment. 'Goodnight, Gus.'

Just like that, their meeting was over. No peck on the cheek. Not even a handshake. Clearly, no bridges would be built tonight.

Maybe never.

With a polite nod, Gus turned and, without hurrying, he moved decisively and with a distinct sense of purpose, away from her, up the stairs and into the hotel.

CHAPTER THREE

Gus downed a Scotch from the minibar, then ordered a room service meal. Promptly, a box of Singapore noodles arrived and he ate lounging on the bed, watching National Rugby League live on TV. The Roosters were playing the Dragons and normally he'd be riveted, not wanting to miss one tackle or pass.

Tonight he was too restless to pay attention. The best he could hope was that the charging footballers and the voices of the commentators would provide a familiar and reassuring background to his rioting thoughts.

He was out of luck.

Before the game reached half-time, he set his meal aside, grabbed the remote and switched the TV off. Pushing the sliding glass doors open, he went out onto the balcony and looked out at the shimmering stretch of dark water.

Breathing deeply, he told himself that he *had*

to let go of his anger. Anger wasn't going to help
Nick. The only way he could help the boy was to
give him his kidney, although at this stage even
that wasn't guaranteed.

The boy might die.

Despair threatened to overwhelm him. He
fought it off by concentrating on the positives
of this situation. He was in a position to volun-
teer his help. He was fit and healthy and in the
right blood group and he would donate the organ
gladly. From what he'd heard about these trans-
plants, there was every chance they'd have a good
result.

He just wished he could let go of the hurt he
felt whenever he thought about the eleven and a
half years that Nick had been on this earth.

In many ways he felt as if he'd been living a lie.
Not only had he married another woman, but he'd
spent those years working hard to help people in
Africa, to give them better lives. He'd even managed to feel noble at times, but all the while, here
in Australia, he'd had a son he'd done nothing
for.

There could be no doubt that the boy was

his. Freya wouldn't have come looking for him otherwise.

But it was so hard to accept that he'd made his girlfriend pregnant and then she'd chosen not to tell him.

It was even harder to accept the reasons Freya had given him for keeping her pregnancy secret—that she'd felt unworthy, or a nuisance, or just plain unsuitable for him.

Looking at it another way, he'd been deemed unworthy for a role most men expected as their right.

Thoughts churning, Gus stared at the harbour. In total contrast to his turmoil, the water was still and calm, reflecting the smooth silvery path of the moon. His thoughts zapped back to Africa, to the many nights he'd sat on the veranda of his Eritrean hut with Monique, his wife, eating traditional flatbread and spicy beef or chicken, while looking out at this very same moon.

He wondered what Monique would have thought about his situation.

Actually, he knew exactly how she'd have reacted. As a doctor with a fierce social con-science, she would have expected him to donate

a kidney without question. She would have sup-
ported the transplant, if she'd still been alive and
married to him. Monique was a pragmatist and
his illegitimate son from a previous girlfriend
wouldn't have fazed her. She'd had a realistic,
unromantic attitude to relationships.

Once, he would have said that Monique and
Freya were polar opposites. His wife had been a
practical scientist and aid worker, while his first
girlfriend was a romantic and dreamy artist. After
tonight, he wasn't so sure. Freya, the romantic
artist, had made a very hard-headed decision
twelve years ago.

A heavy sigh escaped Gus as he looked at the
rocks where he'd sat earlier tonight with her.

Freya, the siren.

There'd always been an element of enchantment
in his attraction to her, and it seemed she still had
the power to cast a spell over him. This evening,
sitting on those rocks, listening to her explanations in her soft, musical voice, he'd almost fallen
under her spell again.

He'd become enchanted by visual details he'd
almost forgotten—the way she held her head, the
neat curl of her ear, the way she smiled without

showing her slightly crooked front tooth. Hers was a natural beauty that no amount of fashion sense or make-up could achieve, and she'd always had a kind of fantasy mermaid aura.

There were no salon-induced streaks or highlights in her long silky hair and her clothing was utterly simple—a slim-fitting plain sleeveless shift in a hue that matched her eyes—somewhere between misty-green and blue.

Her only jewellery had been an elegant string of cut glass beads, again in blues and greens, which she wore around one slim tanned ankle.

Gus remembered that she'd always worn anklets when she was young and this evening, despite his anger and shock, he'd found this one disturbingly attractive. He'd felt the same helpless stirrings of attraction he'd felt at eighteen, and he'd seen a look in her eyes that had sent his blood pounding. He'd almost been willing to forgive her for not telling him about Nick.

Then she'd dropped her bombshell about the boy's illness and he'd understood that this meeting was not a voluntary move to reunite father and son. It was simply a search for an organ donor and, without that desperate need, Freya might never have told him.

Suddenly, there'd been so much anger raging inside him he doubted he could ever forgive her.

Should he try?

Wasn't it too much to ask?

A cloud arrived quickly, covering the moon, and the silver path on the water vanished. Wrapped in darkness, Gus felt unbearably lonely. Alienated. Angry. So angry it blazed like a bushfire in his gut.

But tangled up with the anger was niggling guilt.

If only he'd been more perceptive on that day Freya had come to him. Why hadn't he realised how insecure she'd felt? And, when she'd stopped answering his mail, why hadn't he gone back to Sugar Bay to demand a response?

Instead, he'd listened to his mates, who'd embraced the plenty more fish in the ocean philosophy, and he'd let his relationship with his schoolboy crush fizzle out.

The weight of those choices wrenched a groan from Gus. But it was too late for regrets and, no matter where the blame lay, the one person who mattered now was his son.

He had to make sure that Nick didn't suffer because of his anger. Hell, he could remember what it was like to be eleven going on twelve, all the frustrations, the hopes, the energy and the awkwardness. And he hadn't been facing the prospect of kidney failure.

That thought sent a cold chill snaking over his skin. Sickening desperation gripped him and he prayed that he was a suitable donor. But then he reasoned that, if all went well and he was a match for Nick, he and Freya and their son would find themselves caught up in an even deeper whirlpool of emotions.

So it made sense from the outset to have a very clear plan of how he would negotiate the pitfalls.

Watching the moon shimmer faintly from behind the cloud, he made a decision. He would do whatever was in his power to help his son, but he would maintain a clear emotional distance from the boy's mother. He had to accept that he would always find Freya attractive. Spending time with her, being close to her would be sweet torture, but he mustn't contemplate revisiting temptation.

The last thing their boy needed now was the distraction of estranged parents trying to recapture their youth.

Gus had made all kinds of wrong assumptions about Freya when they were young, and this time he wanted no confusion. He was always prepared to admit his mistakes, but he prided himself on never making the same mistake twice.

Normally, Freya didn't mind dining alone.

Although she'd had several almost-serious boyfriends, she was well and truly used to being seen in public without an escort. This evening, however, when the waitress in the hotel's bistro showed her to a table for two, then removed the extra place setting, Freya felt unusually conspicuous.

It was ridiculous, but she felt as if everyone in the room could guess that she'd invited a man to dine with her and he'd turned her down.

But, in all honesty, she wasn't sure if she was relieved or disappointed that Gus had declined her invitation.

She knew she should be relieved. She'd won

Gus's cooperation but he was going to keep his distance, which meant she would be spared any unnecessary complications. It was, really, the best possible outcome.

Too bad for her that seeing Gus again had stirred up all sorts of longings and heartaches. Too bad that she kept remembering the warmth of his hands, and the deep rumble of his voice, and the exact shape of his curvy, kissable mouth. It was especially too bad that she could still remember from all those years ago the bone-melting fabulousness of his lips on hers.

She was a fool to think about that now. It would be the worst kind of madness to start falling for Gus again. Surely she'd learned, once and for all, that she wasn't his type.

Her unsuitability had been a painful discovery when she'd visited Gus at university. This evening he'd confirmed it when he told her that the woman he'd loved and chosen as his wife had been a doctor, not just any doctor, but a brave, unselfish, generous woman who worked with the Médecins Sans Frontières. Freya knew she could never live up to such high standards. Not even close.

She had no choice but to squash her romantic memories and to bury them deep, just as she had years and years ago, before Nick was born.

The waitress came back to take Freya's order, but she'd been so lost in the past she hadn't even looked at the menu. Now she gave it a hasty skim-read and ordered grilled coral trout and a garden salad and, because she needed to relax, she also asked for a glass of wine, a Clare Valley Riesling.

Alone again, she sent a text message to Nick reassuring him that she would be home by tomorrow night. She sent her love but she didn't mention the F word.

Father.

When she'd flown to Darwin, she'd merely told Nick she was meeting a 'potential donor.' At this point, she wasn't sure how she was going to handle the next huge step of telling Nick about Gus Wilder.

If only there was a way to tell him gently without the inevitable excitement and unrealistic hope. She knew from bitter experience that meetings with fathers could be hazardous.

* * *

Freya was brisk and businesslike next morning when she phoned Gus. 'I have the doctors' phone numbers and addresses ready for you.'

'Thank you.' He sounded equally businesslike. 'Why don't we meet in the hotel's coffee bar?'

'I'll see you there in five.'

She'd tidied her room in case Gus planned to drop by, but the coffee bar was a sensible alternative—neutral ground, in line with his aim to retain a discreet distance.

She knew she shouldn't have checked her appearance in the mirror—it didn't matter what she looked like—but she did check. Twice. Once to apply concealer to the purple shadows beneath her eyes. The second time to give her hair a final run through with a comb and to add a touch of bronze lip gloss.

When she saw Gus, she noted guiltily that he also had telltale dark smudges under his eyes. *And* there were creases bracketing his mouth that she hadn't noticed yesterday. Even the bones in his face were more sharply defined. Clearly, his night had been as restless and sleep-deprived as hers.

Gus didn't waste time with pleasantries. As soon

as they'd ordered their coffees, he got straight down to business. 'Do you have those contact details?'

Last night, she'd listed everything he needed. Now she retrieved the sheet of paper from her purse and handed it over.

He read the page without comment, then folded it and slipped it inside his wallet. When he looked up again, she was surprised to see the faintest hint of warmth in his dark brown eyes. 'Your handwriting hasn't changed. It's still the curliest, loopiest script I've ever seen.'

Freya risked a brief smile. 'I'm an artist. What do you expect?'

'So you've kept the art up? I've often wondered if you continued with your plans to study painting.'

The word *often* made Freya's heart flutter. Had Gus really thought about her often?

She tried not to let it matter. 'I've studied in dribs and drabs. A part-time course here, an evening class there.'

'It must have been difficult with a baby.'

'I managed. I still paint.'

Their coffees arrived—a soy cappuccino for Freya and a long black for Gus.

As Gus picked up his cup, he asked, super-casually, 'Does Nick have any artistic flair?'

'Oh, no.' With a nervous smile, she selected a slim packet of raw sugar from a bowl of assorted sweeteners, tore off the end and tipped half of the crystals into her coffee. 'Nick's sporty and brainy.'

Avoiding the intense flash in Gus's eyes, she began to stir the sugar. 'He's good at maths and science and football.' Her face grew hot. 'Like you.'

She looked up then and wished she hadn't. The stark pain in Gus's face made her heart thud painfully.

Don't look like that, Gus.

Last night, as she'd tossed and turned, she'd assured herself that it was possible to get through this without becoming too emotionally entangled with him. But was she fooling herself? He'd merely asked one simple question and now she was struggling, on the brink of tears. And she suspected that Gus was too.

Their situation was so delicate and complicated.

They shared a son whose life was in danger, and they shared a past that still harboured a host of buried emotions.

Freya's wounds were twelve years old and she'd thought they were well and truly protected by thick layers of scar tissue, but the smallest prod proved they were still tender. Gus's wounds, on the other hand, were new and raw and clearly painful.

'About the medical tests,' she said quickly, sensing an urgent need to steer their conversation into safer, more practical waters. 'I'm pretty sure you can have them done in Darwin. The hospital can send the results on so, with luck, you shouldn't have too much disruption to your building project.'

Gus dismissed this with a wave of his hand. He frowned. 'What have you told Nick about...about his father?'

'I...I said you were someone I knew when I was young.'

'Does he know my name?'

Freya shook her head and a pulse in her throat began to beat frantically. 'I said you were a...a good man...that you'd spent a lot of time overseas.' Her fingers twisted the half-empty sugar sachet. 'He did ask once, ages ago before he got sick, if he was ever going to meet you. I said it would be better to wait till he's grown up.'

'For God's sake, Freya. Why?'

Unable to meet the blazing challenge in his eyes, she looked away. 'I knew you were in Africa, and I couldn't go chasing after you there. I did look up what was involved and it was terribly complicated.'

Gus looked shocked.

Freya shrugged. 'I…I guess I was waiting for the right time. But then we went through the experience of meeting *my* father, and it was a disaster.'

'What happened?'

'Let's just say it was a bitter disappointment. Very upsetting for all of us.'

Gus let out his breath on a slow huff. 'OK… so…I take it Nick doesn't know you're meeting me now?'

She shook her head.

His jaw tightened. 'Do you have a photo of him?'

'A photo? Oh…um…I…' Freya gulped, swamped by a tidal wave of embarrassment.

'I'd like to see what my son looks like.'

Good grief. Why hadn't she thought to bring a photo? She didn't even carry one in her purse.

She was rarely separated from Nick. His school was just around the corner from her gallery and she hardly ever left the Bay, so she'd never felt the need to carry her son's photo. And, coming here, she'd been so stressed, so focused—her mind was a one-way track.

Saving Nick's life filled her every waking thought.

From over the rim of his coffee cup, Gus was watching her discomfort with a stern lack of sympathy. 'No photo?'

'No…I'm sorry.' How could she have been so thoughtless? 'I'll get photos for you, Gus. Of course, you must have photos. Absolutely. I'll scan the whole album and send them by email just as soon as I get back.'

'When are you flying back to the Bay?'

'This afternoon.'

Gus placed his coffee cup carefully on its saucer and, with his mouth set in a grim line, he leaned forward, arms folded, elbows on the table.

To Freya, the pose made his shoulders look incredibly wide and somehow threatening.

'I'd like to come too,' he said.

Thud. This was *so* not something she'd bargained for. Not today. Not so soon.

'I'm sure you understand that I want to meet my son.' Gus spoke with the quiet but no-nonsense determination he probably used to push aid projects past obstructionist Third World governments.

'You mean you'd like to fly back to the Bay today?'

'Yes… Why not?'

We're not ready. I'm not ready. 'I…I thought you were in the middle of a very important building project.'

'I am, but there's a window of opportunity. The designs are finished, the materials have been ordered and there's another engineer supervising the foundations. So I phoned the site and the elders are happy to shoulder more responsibility for a limited time.'

'Oh, I…see.'

Freya had known from the start that eventually Gus would want to meet Nick, and their meeting would be emotional and wonderful—but terribly complicated. She hadn't dreamed, though, that Gus would want to come back to the Bay with her straight away. She needed time to prepare Nick, to warn him.

She couldn't help remembering her own brief encounter four years ago with her male parent—she shied away from thinking of Sean Hickey as her *father*… Meeting him hadn't been worth it. Nick had learned then, at the age of seven, that happy reunions were also potential disasters.

Gus would be different, almost certainly. But so soon?

Freya found herself grasping at straws. 'There probably won't be any plane seats available at such late notice.'

'There are seats.' A faint smile played on Gus's face, making attractive creases around his eyes.

'You've already checked?'

He pulled a very smart state-of-the-art phone from his pocket.

'I suppose that has Internet connection,' she said faintly.

'Yes. It's so easy.'

In other words, Gus was five steps ahead of her.

'Well…that's…wonderful.' Freya forced enthusiasm into her voice. Which, in all honesty, wasn't so terribly difficult. There had been a time when this possibility had been her secret dream, and she'd longed for Gus Wilder to come back to the Bay. The only problem was that in her fantasy he'd claimed her as well as Nick. He'd been incredibly understanding and considerate, and her secret hadn't been an issue between them.

In her fantasy, Gus had fallen in love with her again and he'd adored Nick and in no time they'd been married and formed a perfect little family.

How pathetic that dream seemed now. Thank heavens she'd come to her senses.

Gus was frowning. 'You don't object to my seeing the boy, do you?'

'No-o-o, of course not.' *Not in theory.*

His eyes narrowed as he studied her. 'But you look worried. Is there a problem?'

Freya shook her head. 'No. No problem. Not if we're careful.'

'I want to help Nick any way I can, Freya.' He watched her for another beat or two, then said quietly, 'I promise I won't rush in and do anything rash.'

Yes. She would make sure of that.

CHAPTER FOUR

IT WAS mid-afternoon when they landed at Dirranvale, a short distance inland from Sugar Bay. After collecting Freya's car from the airport's overnight car park, they drove to the coast along a road that wound through tall fields of sugar cane.

Everything was exactly as Gus remembered— the gentle undulating countryside, the rich red soil, the endless sea of feathery mauve plumes on top of the waving stalks of cane. He was caught by an unexpected slug of nostalgia.

He remembered the first time he'd made this journey at the age of sixteen, slouched beside his sister in the back of his parents' station wagon. Back then, they were both furious about their father's transfer to the Bay, hating that he'd dragged them away from their city school and their friends.

They'd sulked and squabbled throughout the

entire journey from Brisbane…until they'd crested the last rise…and the Bay had lain before them in all its singular, perfect beauty.

Remembering his first sight of the beach town that had been his home for two magical years, Gus felt a ripple of excitement. His nostrils twitched, already anticipating the briny scent of the sea and the tang of sunscreen. He could almost feel the sand, soft and warm under his feet, and the sun's burning heat on his bare shoulders.

He could practically hear the rolling thump and rush of the surf and, for the first time in a very long time, he found himself remembering the out-of-this-world thrill of riding a board down the glassy face of a breaking wave.

He'd loved this place. Why on earth had he taken so long to come back?

He turned to Freya. 'I bet Nick loves living here.'

'Oh, he does. No doubt about that.'

Most of her face was hidden by sunglasses, but Gus saw the awkward pucker of her mouth and he knew she was nervous, possibly even more nervous than he was.

They hadn't talked much on the plane, mainly

because a nosy middle-aged woman who'd sat next to them had tried to join in every conversation.

He'd learned, however, that Nick was staying at Poppy's place while Freya was away, but that Freya and the boy normally lived in a flat attached to an art gallery. They'd agreed that Gus would stay at the Sugar Bay Hotel.

'I suppose you've warned Poppy to expect me?' he asked.

'Actually, no,' Freya said, surprising him. 'I haven't told her yet.' She chewed at her lip.

'Is there a reason you haven't told her? Does she still have a problem with me?'

Not quite smiling, Freya shook her head. 'I knew she wouldn't be able to help herself. She wouldn't have been able to keep the news to herself. She might have told Nick about you, and got him all worked up.'

It was understandable, Gus supposed, given how restless and on edge he'd felt ever since he'd learned about his son. 'So how do you want to handle this? Will I go straight to the hotel and wait to be summoned?'

They'd come to a junction in the road and Freya

concentrated on giving right of way to oncoming traffic before she turned.

When this was accomplished, she answered Gus's question. 'Nick's playing football this afternoon and I thought it might be a good idea if you went to the game.' Quickly she added, 'It would be a more relaxed atmosphere.'

At first Gus was too surprised to speak. All day he'd been trying to imagine meeting his son, and he'd always pictured an awkward introduction indoors with Poppy and Freya hovering anxiously over the whole proceedings. A football match was the last thing he'd expected, but the idea of meeting Nick at a relaxed social event appealed.

'That's smart thinking,' he told her. 'What kind of football does Nick play?'

'Rugby league.'

Gus swallowed against the rapid constriction in his throat. There'd been a time when he'd lived to play rugby league. He'd loved it almost as much as surfing. 'How can Nick play league in his condition? It's such a tough game.'

'I know.' Freya shrugged. 'I thought the doctors would put a stop to it, but they said he's fine to play while his medication's still working.'

'That's amazing.'

'Except…as I told you, the medication has a time limit.'

Gus scowled. 'So when will you tell him who I am, and why I'm here?'

'I don't think we can talk about that sort of thing at the game. We should go back to my place.'

Her place.

Unreasonably, that cold feeling of exclusion encircled Gus again. Freya and Nick had a home where they'd lived as a special unit for all these years. Without him.

It was only then that he realised they were cresting the last rise—and suddenly there was the Bay lying below them, even more beautiful than he remembered.

Considerately, Freya stopped the car so he could take in the view. The small town hugged the pristine curve of pale yellow sand strung between two green headlands that reached out like arms to embrace the sparkling, rolling sea.

'Wow.' He hadn't dared to hope that it might still be the sleepy seaside village he remembered. 'It hasn't changed.'

'Not too much.'

'I was worried the beach would be crawling with tourists by now, or spoiled by developers.'

'There are a lot more houses.' Freya waved to the cross-hatching of streets and rooftops that stretched back from the beachfront. 'And there are new blocks of units on The Esplanade.'

She pointed out a handful of tall buildings that stood, boldly out of place, near the shops overlooking the sea. 'The local councillors have been very strict, though. They won't allow any building taller than six floors.'

'Good thinking.'

Disconnected memories came rushing back. Eating fish and chips on the beach straight from the paper they were wrapped in. Watching the flashes of summer lightning out to sea. Surfing the waves and feeling at one with the forces of nature, with the whole universe.

That last summer, which he'd forever thought of as Freya's summer.

Gus felt as if a thorn had pierced his heart.

Freya started up the car again and, as they headed down the hill, he saw the house his parents had owned, perched on a clifftop overlooking the bay. Lower down, they reached the suburban streets where many of their friends had lived, and then the high school, with the new addition of an impressive brick gymnasium.

Neither Gus nor Freya spoke as they continued on two blocks beyond the school to the football field ringed by massive banyan trees.

Gus stared through the windscreen and his throat was tighter than ever as he glimpsed the grassy sports oval between the trees. He saw the white timber goalposts, the young boys in colourful jerseys, the rows of parked cars and the players' friends and families gathered along the sidelines, or sitting on folding chairs in the shade.

For two happy years, this had been his world.

Now it was his son's world.

The picture swam before him and he was forced to blink.

Freya turned off the engine.

'How are you feeling?' he asked her.

'I'm a bit shaky.'

Gus nodded. Shaky was exactly how he felt. This was such a big moment. Huge. Almost as momentous and huge as getting married, or witnessing a birth. Twelve years too late, he was about to become a father.

A roar erupted from the crowd as they got out of the car and Freya sent a quick glance over her shoulder to the field.

'Looks like the other team has scored a try.' She pouted her lower lip in mock despair.

'Who's the opposition?'

'Dirranvale. They usually beat us.'

'Nothing's changed, then.' Gus sent her a quick grin, and he was rewarded by an answering grin.

Wow.

Wow. Wow. Wow. Even when Freya's face was half hidden by sunglasses, the grin transformed her. She was the laughing beach girl of his past, and his heart leapt and rolled like a breaking wave.

Impulsively, he reached an arm around her shoulders, moved by an overpowering urge to plant a deep, appreciative kiss on her smiling mouth.

Just in time, he remembered that she'd chosen to keep him out of her life, out of his son's life, and he stamped down on the impulse.

Just as well. Freya wouldn't have welcomed it. Even his casual hug troubled her. Her lips trembled, her smile disintegrated and she moved away, leaving his arm dangling in mid-air.

Fool. Gus shoved his hands in his pockets. He was here to meet Nick, to *save* Nick. Flirting with the boy's mother was not an option. Neither of them wanted to rake up out-of-date emotions and he'd promised himself he wouldn't put a foot wrong during this visit.

Hurrying ahead of him, Freya had already reached the sideline and some of the bystanders turned, smiled and waved to her or called hello. As Gus joined her, they eyed him with marked curiosity, but he paid them scant attention. His interest was immediately fixed on the team of boys in the blue and gold Sugar Bay jerseys.

His son was one of those boys.

Right now, they were standing in a disconsolate row, watching as the opposition's goal kicker booted the ball over the bar and between the posts. The whistle blew, the Dirranvale team's score jumped another two points, then both teams regrouped, ready to resume the game.

Fine hairs lifted on the back of Gus's neck.

'Where's Nick?' he murmured to Freya. 'Is he on the field?'

She nodded. 'I bet you'll recognise him.'

Gus felt a spurt of panic. Was he supposed to instantly know which boy was his? Was this some kind of test?

Freya's sunglasses hid the direction of her gaze and his heart thumped as he scanned the field. There were thirteen boys out there in the Sugar Bay jerseys. He had no idea if Nick was dark or fair, tall or thickset, if he took after the Wilder family or the Joneses.

Should he be looking for a kid who was frailer than the rest? Or was his son the chubby kid, red-faced and panting and avoiding the ball?

The Sugar Bay team had possession of the ball and parents yelled instructions from the sidelines. The boys were running down the field, throwing passes, trying to make ground and dodge being tackled. As far as Gus could see, they were all happy and healthy and bursting with energy. It was hard to believe that any one of them could be seriously ill.

The boy in the number seven jersey suddenly broke ahead of the pack. He had a shock of black hair and dark grey eyes, and there was something about his face. Gus felt a jolt, a lightning bolt of connection. *Recognition?*

'I don't suppose that could be him, could it?' His voice was choked. 'Number seven?'

'Yes, that's Nick!' Freya's cry was close to a sob and she stood beside him with her arms tightly crossed, hugging her middle.

Nick. His kid. Nicholas Angus. Gus felt a rush of adrenaline as he watched the boy and he tried to pinpoint why he was so familiar. Apart from colouring, they weren't really alike.

But there was *something.*

Gus's eyes were riveted on Nick's dashing dark-haired figure as he cleverly sidestepped an attempted tackle, then passed the ball.

He was good. Hey, Nick was really good. He moved forward again, ready for another chance to take possession, and Gus couldn't suppress a fierce glow of pride.

The kid was fast. He was a halfback, a key position in any team, requiring speed and ball-playing skills and a quick mind rather than brute strength.

Chest bursting, Gus watched as Nick took the ball once more and passed it on neatly and deftly, a split second before he was tackled to the ground.

Gus elbowed Freya's arm. 'You didn't tell me he was terrific.'

Her mouth pulled out of shape, halfway between a happy grin and heartbreak.

And suddenly Gus felt as if he'd swallowed the damn football. He looked away, staring into the canopy of one of the ancient trees as he willed his emotions into some kind of order. Once the game was over, he would meet Nick and he'd have to play it cool.

But it was such a massive thing to know that this wonderful kid was his child. He was flooded by a rush of emotion—of responsibility, of happiness and pride—and all of it tangled with fear and the weight of loss for all the years he'd been deprived of this pleasure.

If I'd seen him in the street I would have walked straight past and totally ignored him.

Knowing made such a difference.

But there was so much more he wanted to know. How could he and Nick possibly bridge all their missing years?

* * *

Freya thought she might burst with the tension.

She'd hoped that viewing the game from the sidelines would be an easier induction for Gus, giving him the chance to take a good long look at Nick before he had to cope with introductions. But *she* wasn't finding it easy at all. With each minute that passed, she was more on edge.

She'd watched Nick play football many times, but she usually chatted with other mums and paid only fleeting attention to what was happening on the field. Today, she couldn't drag her eyes from her boy, kept trying to see him though Gus's eyes.

She knew she was hopelessly biased, but Nick was gorgeous, with his lovely dark hair and beautiful, soulful, intelligent grey eyes. She couldn't imagine what it must be like for Gus to be seeing his son for the first time.

She remembered her own introduction to Nick. All those years ago.

With Poppy at her side as her birthing coach, there'd been gentle music playing in the background and the scents of lavender aromatherapy candles. Poppy had helped Freya to breathe through her contractions and, although the whole process was hard work, Nick's arrival had been a calm and beautiful experience.

And he was perfect. Eight and a half pounds, with lovely dark hair, sturdy limbs and great energetic lungs.

It was only later, after Poppy and the midwife left Freya alone to rest, that she'd allowed herself to cry.

She'd cried for Gus.

And she'd cried oceans. She'd missed him so terribly, and she'd longed for him to see their baby. She'd cried and cried so hard and for so long that the nurse had called the doctor, who'd come hurrying back, and he'd been worried and wanted to prescribe a sedative.

Freya had been breastfeeding and she was sure a sedative couldn't be good for her baby, so she'd rallied. From her first days as a mother, she'd always put Nick's needs first.

But, because she'd managed just fine without ever meeting her dad, she'd convinced herself that her son could manage without a father. She'd told herself that she would unite the boy and his dad once Nick was old enough to understand…but by then Gus had been in the depths of Africa.

Freya was so wrapped in her worries she hadn't even realised that the game was over until she saw the boys on the field shaking hands and reaching for water bottles. It was obvious from their body language that the Sugar Bay team had lost.

She glanced quickly at Gus. His body language spoke volumes too. He was so tense he was practically standing to attention.

Out on the field, Nick's coach, Mel Crane, was giving the boy a pat on the back. Nick turned and saw Freya and he grinned and waved, called to his team-mates, then began to jog across the field towards her.

Nick was halfway to them before he saw Gus and his pace slowed. By contrast, Freya's heart began to canter. She took deep breaths, trying to calm down, and she stifled a longing to reach for Gus's hand. How crazy would that be? Gus was here to help Nick, and for no other reason.

She mustn't give the impression that she needed him too. And she certainly mustn't send Nick mixed messages about her relationship with his father. There must be no confusion.

Beside her, Gus dipped his head and spoke close to her ear. 'I'll take my cues from you.'

She nodded and pinned on a smile. *Always assuming I know how to handle this.* Problem was, etiquette advice didn't cover this kind of introduction.

Nick didn't run into Freya's arms as he might have done a few years ago, but he let her kiss him. He smelled hot and dusty and sweaty and she relished the smell—the scent of a normal, healthy eleven-year-old footballer.

'You were fantastic,' she told him, as she told him after every game. 'And you'll beat them next time, for sure.'

Nick accepted this with a smiling shrug. Then he shot a curious glance at Gus.

Freya jumped in quickly. 'Nick, this is Gus Wilder. He's come back from Darwin with me.'

Nick's dark eyes widened and a mixture of tension and curiosity crept into his face. 'Hi,' he said.

'How do you do, Nick?' Gus's deep voice held exactly the right note of friendly warmth. He held out his hand and Freya's heart tumbled as her son and his father exchanged a manly handshake.

'You made some great plays out there,' Gus said.

'Thanks.' Nick grinned, clearly warmed by the praise. He looked at Freya, his eyes flashing questions. Dropping his voice, he asked, 'Is Mr Wilder—'

'You can call him Gus, Nick. He's a friend.' Conscious of the people milling around them, Freya chose her words carefully. 'He's hoping to be a good match for you.'

'Really?' Nick's grin widened and this time when he looked at Gus, his eyes absolutely glowed. 'Wow!'

Gus's eyes glowed too as he cracked a shaky smile.

'So how did you find—'

'Hey, Gus, is that you?' a voice called from behind them. 'Gus Wilder?'

Mel Crane, the football coach, was an old class-mate from Sugar Bay High and he grinned madly and slapped a beefy hand on Gus's shoulder. 'Thought it was you. Good to see you, mate.'

'Mel, how are you?'

'Not bad. Not bad. What brings you back to the Bay? Are you here for long?'

Gus's smile was guarded. 'Just a short trip.'

Mel Crane's pale blue eyes flickered with keen

interest, and Freya's anxiety levels began to climb. As Nick's coach, Mel was one of the few people in the Bay who knew about the boy's condition. He also knew that Freya and Gus had once been an item.

It wouldn't be long before he put two and two together.

'Young Nick played a terrific game today.' Mel ruffled the boy's hair. 'But you know, Nick, Gus here was a *great* footballer.' He gave Gus another hearty thump on the shoulder. 'Lucky for me, he was also good at maths. He used to let me copy his homework.'

Nick laughed and Freya could see that his admiration for Gus was rapidly escalating to hero worship.

'How do you know my mum and my coach?' Nick asked Gus. 'Did you used to live here?'

'Ages ago,' Gus said, carefully avoiding Freya's eyes. 'But I only lived here for a couple of years. Last two years of high school.'

Stepping in quickly before too many memories were laid bare, Freya said, 'I'm afraid we're going to have to whisk Gus away now, Mel. We want to catch a few of the sights before it gets dark.'

'Yeah, sure,' Mel said. 'If you've got a spare moment while you're here, Gus, drop in to the garage.'

'Still the same place down on The Esplanade?'

'Yep. My brother Jim and I have taken over from the old man.'

Gus shook Mel's hand. 'I'm staying at the hotel. I'll call in.'

'Lovely,' said Freya quickly. 'I think we'd better get going now.' Keen to avoid being held up by anyone else, she shepherded Nick and Gus ahead of her to the car.

The worst wasn't over yet.

For Gus, it felt surreal to be sitting in the car beside Freya, with their son in the rear, unaware that his life was about to change for ever.

'So what sights do you want to see, Gus?' Nick asked, leaning forward eagerly.

Gus shot Freya a questioning glance.

'I think we should go straight home,' she said.

'But you told Mr Crane—'

'I know what I told Mr Crane, Nick, but I needed

an excuse to get away. I want to take Gus back to our place. There's a lot to talk about.'

'About the kidney?'

'Yes.'

Nick flopped back in his seat and stopped asking questions. In the stretch of silence, Gus stole a glance back over his shoulder and found the boy watching him, his eyes huge and wondering. Gus sent him a smiling wink. Nick smiled shyly, and Gus felt his heart turn over.

Freya turned the car onto The Esplanade, where late afternoon shadows stretched across the beach. Sunbathers were packing up but a handful of hardy board riders were still catching waves. He watched them. He'd been like them once, not wanting to leave the water till it was almost dark, much to his mother's consternation.

To his surprise, he saw that Freya was turning into a driveway. 'Do you live here? Right on the beachfront?'

'Where else?' A quick smile flitted across her features, but it disappeared in a hurry and Gus knew she was nervous again.

The driveway ran next to a modern building of timber and glass. He caught sight of a sign in the front garden, with *The Driftwood Gallery* painted in pale tan on a cream background.

'Hey, Urchin!' A doggy blur and a wagging tail greeted Nick as they got out of the car. After giving the dog a rough and enthusiastic hug, the boy called to his mother, 'I'm starving.'

'Nothing new there,' Freya responded with an elaborate roll of her eyes.

Gus retrieved their overnight bags from the boot while Freya opened bi-fold doors, and he followed her into an open-plan living area.

'Hey, this is beautiful,' he said, looking around him.

'Not bad, is it?' She dumped her purse and keys on a granite topped counter. 'I manage the gallery, and this flat is part of the deal. Please, take a seat and I'll make some coffee. Is plunger coffee OK?'

'Yes, perfect, thanks.'

Gus remained standing, taking in details of the off-white walls, gleaming pale timber floors and large picture windows looking out to the sea.

The place felt perfect for Freya. It was so much like her—close to the beach and decorated simply but beautifully in neutral tones with soft touches of peach or sea-green. The colours were repeated in the watercolours that hung on the walls and there was a wistful elegance about the paintings that made him wonder if they were hers.

Nick was at the fridge and helping himself to a brightly coloured sports drink. 'What can I have to eat?'

'The usual,' Freya told him. Already, she'd filled a kettle and switched it on and was retrieving the makings of a sandwich. She shot Gus a quick apologetic smile. 'Excuse us for a moment, please.'

'Of course. You have to feed the hungry beast.'

Nick grinned at him and came to the counter beside his mother, took slices of cheese from a packet and added them to the bread she'd buttered.

'I hope you've washed your hands.'

'Washed them at the sink just now.'

'Would you like tomato with this?'

Nick shook his head. 'Cheese is fine.' He added an extra slice, then fetched a plate for his sandwich.

They looked so at home, Gus thought. This

routine was so familiar to them, and his outsider status washed over him like a physical pain.

As if sensing how he felt, Freya said, 'What about you, Gus? Are you hungry? Would you like a sandwich?'

He smiled. 'No, thanks. Coffee's fine.'

Leaning against the counter, plate in hand, Nick munched on his snack. He was still wearing his football gear and Gus saw green smears where he'd landed heavily on the grass, and there was a graze on his knee.

How the hell can this kid be sick? Gus thought. *He looks so normal.*

It seemed so wrong. So cruel.

'So has Mum told you all about my global warning?' the boy asked suddenly, smiling between mouthfuls.

Gus's stomach took a dive. 'Yes, it's rotten luck, but I'm hoping we can turn that around.'

Freya, in the middle of retrieving coffee mugs from an overhead cupboard, appeared to freeze.

'Awesome,' said Nick. 'So do you have O blood, the same as me?'

'I do.'

'But Gus still has to have more tests before we

can be absolutely sure he's a perfect match,' Freya countered.

Nick nodded and looked thoughtful as he chewed again on his sandwich, while the kitchen filled with the smell of coffee.

Across the silence, Gus met Freya's gaze. She sent him a wobbly smile.

'If you could help to carry these things, we can make ourselves comfortable,' she said.

'Sure.' Immediately he snapped into action, and they carried the pot and mugs, a milk jug and a plate of pecan cookies to a low coffee table set amidst comfortably grouped squishy armchairs upholstered in cream linen.

'You want me to hang around?' Nick asked.

Freya's throat rippled as she swallowed. 'Yes, honey, of course. We need to talk to you.'

He came and perched on the arm of one of the chairs, sports drink in one hand, plate with the remains of his sandwich in the other, and he frowned as he watched his mother pour coffee. 'So did you guys know each other before? When Gus used to live here?'

'Yes.' Freya's voice was a shade too tight.

Nick stared at her and his face sobered. He slid

a quick look to Gus, then another glance back to his mother. 'You're not going to tell me anything really crazy, are you? Like Gus is my father or something?'

CHAPTER FIVE

FREYA almost dropped the coffee pot. It clattered onto the table and Gus was instantly attentive.

'Did you burn yourself?'

She shook her head. She was too mortified by Nick's question to worry about the stinging patch of skin on the inside of her wrist. She wished she could think more clearly, wished she could find the right words so that everything made instant sense to Nick. And she wanted to defend Gus.

When she opened her mouth, nothing emerged.

She looked helplessly at Nick, who was watching her and Gus with his lips tightly compressed and a look of anguish in his eyes, as if he wished he could bite back his words.

I have to answer him.

But, as she struggled to find the words, she heard Gus's voice above the fierce hammering of her heartbeats.

'That's exactly right, Nick.' Gus spoke quietly, calmly. 'I've come here because I'm your father and I'm the best person to help you. I want to help you.'

There…

It was out.

Thank you, Gus. Freya felt relief, but a sense of failure too. She should have been ready for this. She knew exactly what her son was like, knew he was smart and perceptive.

When at last she found her voice, she hurried to make amends for her silence. 'Gus really wants to help you, darling. We know there could be other donors, but Gus is your best chance for a really good match.'

A bright red tide was creeping up Nick's neck and into his cheeks. His eyes shimmered with tears.

The sight of his tears tore at Freya's heart. She felt lost. Totally thrown.

Slowly, her son slid from the arm of the chair and he set his plate and drink down on the coffee table.

'Thanks,' he said shakily, not quite meeting anyone's gaze. 'That's great.' Then he shot a nervous glance to Freya. 'If it's OK, I'm going to get changed and take a shower.'

This was so not what she'd expected, so out of character. Nick hardly ever volunteered to have a shower. Freya usually had to shove him into the bathroom. Now, she felt compelled to let him go.

The adults watched in uncomfortable silence as the boy walked from the room, sports shoes squeaking on the polished floors. Neither of them spoke nor moved until they heard Nick's bedroom door close down the hallway.

Freya let out a soft groan. 'That went well.' She felt terrible for Gus. What must he be thinking? Of her? Of their son? 'I'm sorry, Gus. That wasn't quite the reception I imagined.'

'Do you want to go and speak to him?'

'I don't know,' she said, feeling dazed. 'I'm not sure it would help. I…I'll try.' Her legs felt as weak as limp rope when she stood. 'Won't be a moment.'

She went down the hall and knocked on Nick's door. 'Nick?'

'I'm getting undressed.'

'Do you want to talk?'

She heard the thump of his shoes hitting the floor. 'Later.'

'Don't be long,' she called.

When she went back into the living room, Gus gave an easy non-judgemental shrug.

'The boy's had a shock.'

'But you've come all this way to meet him.'

To her surprise, Gus didn't seem angry.

'All in good time,' he said smoothly. 'Nick needs a chance to get his head around everything.'

Gus would know what Nick was going through, of course. He'd had a similar shock less than twenty-four hours ago.

As Freya picked up the coffee pot again, she gave him a grateful smile. 'So…would you still like a cuppa?'

He was staring at her arm, frowning. 'You *did* burn yourself.'

She'd been trying to ignore the stinging, but now she looked down and saw the angry red welt on the pale skin of her inner wrist.

'You need to get something on that,' he said. 'Do you have burn cream?'

'Oh—I have some of Poppy's aloe vera growing in a pot. That'll fix it.'

Frowning, Gus rose and followed her into the kitchen, watching as she snapped off a piece of succulent herb growing on the windowsill.

'Here, let me,' he said, taking the aloe vera from her. 'That will be hard to manage one handed.'

Before Freya could protest, he was holding her arm, gently, ever so kindly. He squeezed the plant to break up the juicy fibres and began very gently to rub it over her reddened skin.

His touch sent an electric shiver trembling through Freya. She was remembering a time when they were young, when she'd had a coral cut on her ankle, and Gus had been so caring—just like this—washing the cut clean and making sure she got antiseptic straight onto it.

OK, so he's a caring guy. I know that. It's why he's here. It's why he's been working in Africa for all these years. That's no excuse for swooning.

'Thanks,' she said extra brightly when he was done. 'That's feeling better already. Now, about that coffee—'

Gus was still holding her arm. She was still flashing hot and cold. And when she looked into his eyes, she saw a look she remembered from all those years ago.

An ache blossomed inside her, treacherous and sweet, and she almost fell into his arms.

He let her wrist go and said, 'I'd love a coffee.'

Just like that, the moment was gone and, as Freya crashed back to earth, she wondered if she'd imagined that look.

She went back to the coffee table, filled their mugs and handed one to Gus.

He sat down and took a sip and made an appreciative noise. 'I remember now. You make very good coffee.'

She smiled faintly and sat very still, holding her coffee mug without tasting it, thinking about Nick, and Gus and…the repercussions of the decision she'd made all those years ago.

From down the hallway came the sound of a shower turning on. Freya and Gus exchanged cautious glances.

'I'd always planned to warn him, to get him ready before he met you,' she said defensively. 'But you insisted on meeting him today.'

Gus sent her a strange look and took another sip of coffee. 'You said Nick had a bad experience when he met your father.'

'Yes. I think it's safe to say he was quite disillusioned.'

'Do you mind telling me what happened?'

She let out a slow huff. 'Well…my father turned up here a few weeks before Christmas. He sailed into the Bay in a pretty little yacht called *Poppy*.' She rolled her eyes. 'You can picture it, can't you? All smart white paint and lovely tanned sails.'

'Like a romantic fantasy,' Gus suggested.

'Exactly.'

'What's his name?'

'Sean Hickey.' Freya drank some of her coffee, then settled back in her chair, as if getting ready to tell a long story. 'He certainly looked the part, all lean and sunburned, with a weather-beaten sailor's tan. Quite handsome, actually, in a wicked, boyish way. White curly hair and bright blue eyes—*and* a charming Irish lilt to his voice.'

'How did Poppy react to seeing him?'

'Oh, she welcomed him with open arms, and she seemed to grow ten years younger overnight. Nick adored him, of course. I mean, he had another male in his family for starters.'

As she said this, she felt a stab from her guilty conscience. She'd always felt bad about denying her son a male role model. 'Nick was seven at the time, and he was over the moon. Sean was the ideal grandfather—lively and friendly and full of fun, and very interested in his grandson.'

Gus regarded her steadily. 'And you?'

'Oh, I was beyond excited too. I had a father, at last.' She avoided Gus's eyes as she said this and her cheeks grew uncomfortably hot. She stumbled on, hoping to make amends. 'Admittedly, Sean wasn't quite the way I'd pictured my father.'

'I seem to remember,' said Gus dryly, 'that you had a list of famous Australians who might have been your father.'

The heat in Freya's face deepened. Gus hadn't forgotten. She, however, had conveniently pushed that memory underground, hadn't let herself think that Nick might feel equally deprived. Or worse.

'Well, Sean wasn't a film star,' she said tightly. 'He was more like a charming pixie, but he lavished praise on my paintings and I lapped it up. He even told me about an artistic grandmother who still lives in County Cork in Ireland.'

Gus smiled. 'So that's where your talent comes from.'

'I'm not sure any more.' Freya shrugged. 'Anyway, he taught Nick how to sail, and he took the three of us out in *Poppy*, and we sailed to the islands and had lovely picnics. He even painted Poppy's house for her.' This was said with an accompanying eye roll. 'Do you remember how Mum's cottage used to look?'

'Of course. It was fabulous. The only house right on the edge of the sand. And painted every colour of the rainbow. It was a talking point in Sugar Bay.'

'Yes, well...wait till you see it now.'

'Why? What did Sean do to it?'

'Painted it white.'

'The whole house?'

She nodded. 'Spanking white with neat aqua blue trims. Spotless and tidy, just like his boat.'

'My God. *Spotless* and *tidy* are two words I'd never associate with Poppy. Did she hate it?'

Freya gave another shrug. 'She pretended to love it. She was smitten at the time, though, so her judgement was clouded.'

'But I take it your dad eventually blotted his copybook?'

'Oh, yes. Big time. A week before Christmas

he totally blackened his name. He and his little yacht just disappeared into the wide blue yonder.' Freya paused significantly. 'Along with Poppy's savings.'

It was gratifying to watch Gus's jaw drop.

'How did he manage that?'

'Oh, you know Poppy. Didn't trust banks, and didn't worry much about money. What little she did accumulate she kept at home in a ginger jar.' Freya sighed. 'It was the gloomiest, most depressing Christmas ever. We tried to be cheerful for poor Nick's sake, but we weren't very good at it, I'm afraid.'

Leaning forward, she put her coffee mug back on the table. 'I found out later from one of the local fishermen that Sean had moved on, up to Gladstone. He'd changed the name of his yacht to *Caroline*, and he was living with a new woman, a widow named Mrs Keane. *Caroline* Keane, of course. *And* he showed no sign of an Irish accent.'

'So he was a con artist.'

'Through and through. And Poppy admitted later that he'd always had a gambling addiction. She'd known that, and she still wasn't careful.'

Gus let out his breath in a whoosh, then rose and paced to the big picture window and stood with his hands resting lightly on his hips as he looked out to sea. 'I see why fathers have a bad name around here.'

Freya stood too and followed him across the room. 'I know you're nothing like Sean, Gus. In fact, you'rc thc opposite. You've come here to give, not to take.'

'That's certainly the plan.' He didn't turn from the window. Outside, it was almost dusk and the sea and the sky had turned a deep pearlescent grey.

'I know Nick liked you, straight off,' Freya said. 'Actually, I'm sure he wants to get to know you. He's just—'

'Scared.'

'Yes.' *We're both scared.*

Trouble was, though Gus might not be a con man, he still had his own special brand of dangerous charm. If he entered their lives, even for a short time, and then left again, as he must, he would almost certainly leave a huge raw-edged hole.

Gus turned from the window. 'I guess I should

head off now. You need to talk to Nick, and I need to book into the hotel.'

'You're welcome to stay here.' Freya had no idea she was going to say that. She was pretty sure Gus wanted to stay in the hotel, to keep an emotional distance, but the invitation had tumbled out spontaneously and she couldn't take it back without looking foolish. She held her breath, waiting for his answer.

To her surprise, his lip curled in a faintly amused smile. 'Don't you think you should consult Nick before making such rash offers? He hasn't exactly welcomed me with open arms, has he?'

'But you're doing a wonderful thing for us, Gus, and we're in your debt. What if I go and talk to him? He's sure to have calmed down by now.'

'Not now, Freya.' Gus wasn't smiling any more. He was deadly serious. 'It will be better for all of us if I stay at the hotel.'

It was ridiculous to feel disappointed. Freya was dredging up a smile when Gus surprised her by reaching for her arm.

'Before I go, let me see that burn. I'm not sure you should trust Poppy's home-grown remedies.'

'Oh, it's fine.' It was true. The burn no longer

stung and, when she looked at her arm, the aloe vera was already working. The angry redness was fading.

Gus's fingers, however, encircled her wrist and, in spite of her beach girl's tan, they looked very dark and strong against her skin. His other hand touched her wrist gently, unbelievably gently. So gently he was killing her.

A tiny gasp escaped her and he went still. She looked up and something in his burning gaze sent a high voltage current through every vein in her body.

She couldn't bear it, had to look away.

He said, 'I'll make contact with Nick's doctor in the morning.'

She was almost too breathless to respond. 'If you need me, I'll be here in the gallery all day.'

'OK. I'll call you.'

Without another word, Gus went to the kitchen door where he'd left his overnight bag. Snagging it with two fingers, he let himself out and he didn't look back.

Freya was chopping mushrooms and onion for a homemade pizza when Nick came into the kitchen. His hair was still wet from his shower, and she always thought he looked younger somehow when his hair was wet. More vulnerable. Tonight, he looked shamefaced too.

He sent a quick glance around their open-plan living area. 'Where's Gus?'

'He's gone to the hotel.' She continued methodically to slice mushrooms.

'Is he buying wine or something for dinner?'

'No, Nick. He's staying at the hotel.'

'Why? Didn't you ask him to stay here?'

Setting down her knife, Freya folded her arms and she sent her son a rueful smile. 'Gus thought it would be better. He wanted to give you time to get over your shock.'

'Oh.'

'He's a good man, Nick. He's not like Sean. He really wants to help you.'

The boy stared at the partly assembled pizza. 'Are you going to put bacon on that?'

'Of course.'

'Plenty?'

'Just the right amount. You know what Dr Kingston said. You're supposed to have lots of vegetables and not too much salt.'

Nick sighed theatrically and, for a moment, Freya thought the subject of Gus had been dropped.

Not so.

Leaning with his elbows on the counter, her son scowled. 'I don't get it. I really don't get it. If Gus is such a great guy, why isn't he a proper father? Why doesn't he live here with us?'

Freya's heart thudded and her brain raced as she searched for the exact words to explain. This moment was so critically important. The explanation was complicated, but she had to get it right.

Clearly, Nick thought she was taking too long and he rushed in with more questions. 'If Gus is so helpful, why'd he go away in the first place? What's wrong with us?' Sudden tears spilled and Nick swiped at them angrily with the backs of his hands. 'What's wrong with our whole freaking family?'

'Oh, darling.' Freya gave up searching for perfect words to answer *these* questions. Instead, she rushed around the kitchen counter to hug him.

* * *

On Monday morning Gus looked out of his hotel window at blue skies and perfect rolling surf and wished his heart felt lighter. He'd spent another restless, unhappy night thinking about Freya and Nick and he'd resolved nothing.

Still yawning, he showered and shaved and went down to the hotel dining room for breakfast. Coffee, fresh fruit and scrambled eggs helped.

Then, as he left the dining room, he came to a sudden, heart-thumping halt. Nick was in the foyer, speaking to a woman at the front desk.

The boy was dressed for school in a blue and white polo shirt with grey shorts and sneakers. He had a school bag slung over his shoulder and he fiddled nervously with its zip while he spoke to the woman behind the counter.

What was he doing here? Gus's heart picked up pace as he hurried forward. 'Nick?'

The boy whirled around. His eyes widened and he smiled nervously. 'Hi, Gus.' He turned back to the desk and said to the woman, 'No need to call the room. It's OK. I've found him.'

I've found him.

The words were like music to Gus, or the world's finest poetry. His son was looking for him. His heart swelled with elation. 'It's good to see you,' he told Nick thickly.

The boy nodded. 'I was hoping I'd find you.'

'Have you had breakfast?' Gus smiled, trying to put the boy at his ease.

'Yes, thanks.' Nick swallowed nervously. 'Mum didn't send me here or anything. I just wanted to see you—to...to talk.'

'Sure. We could go up to my room or—' A glance through the hotel's large plate glass windows showed the beach sparkling in the morning sunshine. 'We could go outside.' Gus smiled again. 'I think I'd rather be out in the fresh air. How about you?'

'Yeah. Outside would be better.'

They went out through automatic sliding glass doors into the pleasant subtropical sunshine. Children zipped past on bikes or dawdled to school. Ubiquitous surfers carrying surfboards mingled with early shoppers strolling on The Esplanade. Gus and Nick walked over soft grass strewn with pine needles to an empty bench seat beneath Norfolk Island pines.

'Look at that.' Gus gestured to the curling waves

and the pristine curve of the beach. 'You know you're lucky to be living here, don't you?'

'Yeah.' Nick smiled shyly. 'But it's not so great when you have to go to school all day.'

'Although…as I remember, the surf's still here when school's out.'

'Yeah, I know.' Nick grinned. 'It's a cool place to live, except lots of people only stay for a while, then move away.' He shot a sideways glance to Gus. 'Like you.'

Making a deliberate effort to appear casual and relaxed, Gus leaned back against the seat's wooden slats and propped an ankle on a knee. 'There aren't a lot of jobs in these parts. That's why people move on. I had to go away to university and then, later, I worked overseas.'

'Yeah, Mum told me.' Nick looked down at his school bag, dumped at his feet, and he reached for the strap, twisting it with tense fingers. 'Like I said, Mum didn't send me here. I told her I had to get to school early. She doesn't even know I'm talking to you.'

Pleased by the boy's honesty, by his obvious concern for Freya, Gus felt a strangely warm glow. 'Maybe we can tell your mum…later.'

'I guess.' Nick kicked at a fallen pine cone. 'We talked last night. About you. Mum told me what happened.'

'Happened—as in—?'

'Why you two split up. She said you didn't deliberately leave us. You didn't even know about me.'

'Well…yes…that's right.'

'And she said it was her decision not to tell you about me.'

Gus couldn't resist asking, 'Did she explain why?'

Nick shrugged. 'Kind of. It didn't really make sense.'

You and me both, kiddo, Gus thought. Even though he understood Freya's motives, her secrecy still hurt, still didn't make proper sense to him. Just the same, he tried to explain it to the boy. 'Sometimes we do things that feel right at the time that don't always make sense when we look back on them later.'

'Especially in my weird family.'

'Trust me, Nick, every family has its own kind of weirdness.'

Wind ruffled the boy's dark hair and he seemed

to consider this for a moment, then shrugged it aside. 'The way Mum tells it—sounds like she wasn't good enough for you.'

Gus lost his casual pose. 'Freya told you that?'

'She didn't say those exact words.'

'But she told you that she couldn't fit into my life?'

'Yeah. Something like that. Sounded pretty lame to me.'

A heavy sigh escaped Gus. How could he ask Nick to understand that he and Freya had been young, that most young people made bad judgements one way or another, although they never felt like mistakes at the time?

The boy was eleven and he couldn't be expected to look on eighteen-year-olds as young, especially when he faced a shockingly uncertain future.

'The good thing is, your mum found me now,' Gus said.

'Yeah. Thanks for coming down here, and offering the kidney and everything.' Nick sent him another shy smile. 'That's actually what I wanted to say.'

Gus smiled back at him. He loved this kid.

Heck, he wanted to wrap his arms around Nick's skinny shoulders and hug him hard. But maybe it was too soon, so he resisted the urge. 'I've got a kidney to spare, and you're welcome to it. But I have to have the tests first.'

'I emailed Dr Kingston last night.'

'You what?'

'Sent him an email,' Nick said nonchalantly.

'I didn't know you could do that.'

'My doctor's pretty cool. And he wrote back to say he's really pleased we found you, and you can get most of your tests done at the Dirranvale hospital, if you want.'

'That sounds good.'

Nick's grey eyes, which were the same shape as Freya's eyes and had the same thick, dark lashes, took on an unexpected twinkle. 'If you're going to Dirranvale, there's something I should warn you about.'

'What's that?'

'One of the nurses up there is a vampire.'

For a split second, Gus wasn't sure how to respond to this. He was about to laugh it off, then he caught the spark of mischief in Nick's grin and changed tack. 'No kidding? A vampire?'

'I reckon when she takes your blood, she keeps some of it for herself.'

'No!' Gus gave an elaborate shudder. 'You'd better describe her to me, so I'll know to avoid her.'

'She's easy to pick. She has long black hair and really, really pale skin.'

'And fangs?'

Nick giggled. 'No. She's actually kind of pretty.'

'Oh, yeah. That would be right. Vampires are often exceptionally beautiful. That's why they're so dangerous. Do you think I should tell her that we know what she's up to?'

Nick's smile lost a little of its certainty. 'I'm not asking you to drive a stake through her heart or anything.'

'Well, that's a relief.' Gus chuckled. 'So you're determined to save her bacon. Does that mean you're keen on her?'

'No way.' The boy went bright pink.

'All right, then. I won't say a word.'

From somewhere in the distance came the ringing of a bell.

'Oh-oh.' Nick scrambled to his feet and scooped up his bag.

'You're going to be late for school.'

'Yeah. I'd better go.'

'You'd better run,' Gus said. 'But be careful crossing the road, won't you?'

'Course.'

'Thanks for the advice about the vampire.'

'Good luck!' Nick flashed a final quick grin, and Gus watched the boy dashing across the grass beneath the pines, dark hair lifting in the breeze, school bag bumping against his hip, and he felt, for a fleeting moment, as if he'd known his son all his life.

Then reality returned like a fist in his guts. He'd been deprived of this fabulous feeling, deprived for the past eleven and a half years.

Freya's concentration was shot to pieces. Gus had phoned to say that he'd hired a car and was driving to Dirranvale for blood tests, X-rays and scans and, although she went through the motions of her normal everyday activities—opening the gallery, smiling at visitors who wandered in, checking mail, answering phone calls—her mind was at the hospital.

She'd been there so many times with Nick and she could picture exactly what Gus was going through—sitting patiently, or perhaps impatiently, on those hard metal seats outside X-ray, then having to change into one of the awful gaping hospital gowns. Afterwards, going on to Pathology to be stuck with needles.

The thought kept her dancing on a knife-edge between hope and fear. This morning, Nick had been so excited, so certain that his dad would save him. He had all his faith pinned on this. And of course she was hoping too…

Even though Nick wasn't in immediate danger, he was on a national waiting list and they'd been assured there would be a donor match out there, but she knew they all, including Gus, wanted him to be the one who gave.

The tissue match had to be perfect, however, so wasn't it foolish to build up too much hope?

She must have whispered *good luck* to Gus at least a thousand times this morning.

When she wasn't doing that, she was thinking about last night and the way Gus had held her wrist and looked at her…She kept seeing the dark shimmer of emotion in his eyes…

The memory filled her head and how crazy was that, to be obsessed by such a teensy, short-lived moment?

It was nothing.

No.

It was something. There'd definitely been *something* happening when Gus had touched her skin… intensity in his face that couldn't be ignored. He'd looked that way all those years ago…on so many occasions during their perfect summer.

Thinking about that summer, Freya found herself drawn into a web of memories…beginning with the first time Gus had asked her out, when he invited her to be his partner at their senior formal.

She could recall every detail of that afternoon in their last year of high school…

Wednesdays always finished with double history, one of the few classes Freya shared with Gus. And on that particular mid-week afternoon he spoke to her just outside the school gate.

Her heart started a drum roll the minute she saw

him standing there and realised he was waiting for her.

She'd been hopelessly smitten from the day Gus arrived at their school two years earlier, but she'd been quite stupidly shy around him and, as Gus had been rather shy too, they'd hardly spoken.

Oh, there'd been a little flirting…and a lot of smiling…but he'd been caught up with his surfing, his football and his studies, and he'd never asked her out on a date. As far as Freya knew, Gus hadn't taken any girl out and there were plenty of girls who'd been hoping.

But, on that special afternoon, he approached her with endearing nervousness.

'Hey, Freya?'

'Hey.' She'd tried to sound casual, as if this wasn't a big deal, like maybe the biggest deal of her life to date…

'I was wondering…if you have a partner for the formal.'

'Um…no, I haven't.' *Oh, God.* Her knees were shaking. 'Not yet.'

Mel Crane shuffled past and sent them a goofy grin.

Gus scowled at him, then offered Freya a shy

tilted smile. 'I was wondering if you'd like to come with me.'

'Um.' Her tongue was suddenly paralysed. *Speak, simpleton!* 'Yes,' she managed at last.

'Yes?' Seemed he was about as inarticulate as she was. Why did he look so disbelieving? As if she wouldn't jump at the chance? His shock gave her courage.

'Yes, Gus, I'd really like to go to the formal with you.'

'Sweet.' He was smiling properly now, smiling fully at her in a way that was a little short of dazzling. 'Terrific. I don't know any details yet, about what time I'll pick you up or anything.'

'That's OK. There's no rush.' She smiled at him bravely. 'Thanks, Gus.'

He walked with her then for three blocks, and she wasn't sure that her feet were touching the ground. They talked about their history teacher, about their friends, about surfing...

When they reached The Esplanade they said goodbye. Their houses were at opposite ends of the Bay.

Oh, man. Freya rushed home to Poppy, bursting with excitement.

And, immediately, she met her first hurdle.

Poppy didn't like the idea of her only daughter going out with a football jock. Weren't they all smart-mouthed thugs? Wasn't there a nice boy Freya could go with? Someone more artistic and sensitive?

Naturally, Freya insisted that Gus was nice. He wasn't just good at football; he was practically top of their class. He was lovely, and she was going with him or with no one.

When Poppy finally, but unhappily, acquiesced, they moved on to the Battle of The Dress.

'I can do wonderful things with a sewing machine and a bucket of dye,' Poppy suggested.

Freya was beyond horrified. She loved her mum, but she flatly refused to go to the formal dressed like a tie-dyed hippie.

'All the other girls are getting their dresses from Mimi's in Dirranvale. Phoebe's mother's even taking her to Brisbane to buy her dress.'

'That girl's mother never had any sense,' Poppy muttered darkly. 'And you know we can't afford so much as a handkerchief from one of those fancy salons.'

'That's OK. I'll earn all the money I need.'

'How?'

'I'll sell aromatherapy candles at the markets.'

Poppy rolled her eyes. She'd gone through her 'market phase', as she called it. She'd sold hand-made soaps and candles and jewellery and she'd made quite good money, but she hated the long hours of constant toil that were required to replenish her stocks week after week, and she'd opted for a part-time job caring for seedlings at a local plant nursery instead.

Freya, however, was determined. She went with her best friend Jane and Jane's mother to Mimi's in Dirranvale and she fell in love with a most divine off-the-shoulder dress and put it on lay-by. Then she gathered used jars from all her neighbours' households and spent hours in the evenings melting wax and adding essential oils and wicks, then decorating the candle jars with silver and gold calligraphy pens.

For a month she spent every weekend doing the rounds of the craft markets in the local seaside towns. She was exhausted, especially as she had to catch the bus back and forth, *and* she had to burn the metaphorical candle at both ends, sitting up till midnight to finish her homework.

But it was worth it. She'd earned enough to buy her dream dress from Mimi's, as well as divine shoes that were dainty enough to make Cinderella jealous, *and* there was money left over for a trip to the hairdresser and a French manicure.

On the night of the formal, Freya slipped into the soft misty-blue chiffon dress that everyone said matched her eyes perfectly. And she felt—amazing!

Gus arrived at her door with a corsage and he looked all kinds of perfect—so tall and dark and handsome in his black tuxedo that Freya thought she might die and go straight to heaven.

And that was *before* they danced, touching each other for the very first time.

CHAPTER SIX

WALKING home with Gus that night was even more sensational than dancing with him. They had to go all the way along the beachfront because Poppy's house was at the far end of the Bay, and it was Freya who suggested they should take off their shoes and walk on the sand.

Gus agreed with gratifying enthusiasm, and they left their shoes beside a pile of rocks. Gus shoved Freya's evening bag into his trouser pocket and rolled up the bottoms of his trousers, while Freya scooped up the hem of her dress in one hand, leaving her other hand free to hold his. *Bliss City!*

If there were other couples on the beach that night, they stayed well in the shadows and Freya and Gus felt quite alone as they strolled hand in hand on the edge of the sand beneath a high, clear sky blazing with stars.

Freya could have stayed out all night. She'd

never felt so happy, so unbelievably alive. She kept wanting to turn to look at Gus. To stare at his gorgeousness. There were so many things she loved about the way he looked—his dark hair with the bit that flopped forward, his deep-set dark eyes, his strong, intelligent profile, his broad shoulders, his long legs, his sturdy hands.

Then there came *that* moment, the moment when Gus let go of her hand and touched the back of her neck.

Freya usually wore her hair down, but that night it was swept up by the hairdresser into a romantic knot.

'Did you know you have the most gorgeous skin right here?'

The feel of Gus's fingers on her nape made her want to curl into his arms.

'I sit behind you in History,' he said. 'And your hair falls forward, and I spend hours admiring the back of your neck.'

'So that's why I get better marks than you in History.'

'Could be.' His fingers stroked just below her hairline. 'I love this bit just here.'

And while she was melting from the touch of his fingers, he touched his lips to her neck.

Freya was shaking. His gentleness was excruciating. She bowed her head, exposing her skin in a silent appeal, begging for more. The touch of his lips on the curve of her neck made her ache deep inside, made her want to cry and to laugh, to dance, to lie down in the shallows.

Then Gus kissed her lips.

Of course it was late when they finally reached her house, especially as they forgot their shoes and had to go back to search for them, and it took ages to remember which pile of rocks they'd left them beside. They were laughing, giggling like children, drunk with happiness.

Gus kissed her again on the front steps. He was still kissing her when Poppy flung the front door open, letting bright light spill over them, and making them blink.

Arms akimbo, her mother glared at Gus.

'Freya should have been home hours ago. Who do you think you are, coming down here and making all sorts of assumptions about my daughter?'

To his credit, Gus was very restrained and

polite, but he left in a hurry. It was Freya who lost her cool, later, after he'd gone.

'How could you be so mean, Mum? We were only kissing. Why did you have to be so awful to Gus?'

'I don't trust him, or any of that snobby lot up on the hill.' Poppy picked up the damp hem of Freya's dress and frowned elaborately at the clinging grains of sand.

'Well, *I* trust him, and surely that's what counts?'

It was an argument that came back to bite Freya four months later, at the end of the summer, after Gus had already left for university in Brisbane and she missed her period.

Now, Freya was so lost in the mists of the past that when the bell at the front door rang, letting her know that yet another visitor had come into the gallery, she didn't look up. Most people liked to be left to wander about looking at paintings without being observed, and she wasn't in the mood for an exchange of happy banter with a tourist.

When a shadow fell over her desk, she

realised she was out of luck. She looked up and heat rushed into her face. 'Gus!'

Gus's heart was pounding, actually pounding. As he'd walked into The Driftwood Gallery, he'd seen Freya sitting at the pale timber desk in the corner. She had her back to him and she was wearing jeans and a grey knitted top that shouldn't have looked sexy, but it was soft and it clung lovingly to her shoulders before falling loosely to her hips, and somehow it managed to look incredibly feminine.

She was leaning forward so that her hair, light brown and streaked with gold, parted like a curtain to show a V of smooth, pale skin on her neck. And suddenly he was remembering every detail of falling in love with Freya Jones and the heady, blinding happiness of that magical summer.

Their summer.

To his dismay, he felt the sting of tears and he found himself recalling all the silly nicknames Freya had given him—Huggy Bear, Hot Stuff, Angel Eyes.

Her favourite had been Sugar Lips, while he'd simply called her Floss.

Memories pulled at him as he approached her desk but, when she looked up, he saw shock in her eyes and then unmistakable fear, and their happy past disintegrated like a jigsaw puzzle breaking up into a thousand separate scattered pieces.

Gus was wrenched back into the present in all its unhappy complexity.

'Hi,' he said, forcing the breezy greeting past the constriction in his throat. Freya's smoky blue eyes were so clouded with worry that he tried to cheer her with a joke. 'I've finally escaped from the evil clutches of the vampire.'

'The vampire?' She looked more worried than ever.

'Hasn't Nick mentioned her?'

'No.'

Damn. Gus grimaced.

'I thought you were at the hospital. What are you talking about?'

'I *have* been at the hospital,' he assured her. 'Every one of my vital organs has been X-rayed and scanned from every conceivable angle, and I've given vast quantities of blood.'

'Oh. Is that the vampire connection?'

'Yeah. Bad joke. But you can blame Nick. He

told me about the vampire nurse when he called in this morning on his way to school.'

'Really?' Freya was on her feet, twisting a locket at her throat with anxious fingers.

'I'm so glad Nick called in to see me, Freya. He came to thank me, and it meant a lot. He's a great kid. You must be proud of him.'

She showed no sign that his words reassured her. She looked distressed and rubbed at her temple, as if her head ached. 'Nick didn't tell me he was going to see you.'

'Well, I think he felt bad about yesterday's reception. And he's entitled to see me. I'm his father, after all.'

'Yes, of course.' She was still frowning and not looking at him.

Gus's jaw tightened. If Freya was going to be a dog in the manger about their son, she'd have a fight on her hands.

'So what will you do now the tests are out of the way?' she asked. 'Will you fly straight back to the Northern Territory?'

'Why?' he asked coldly. 'Are you keen to be rid of me?'

'No. But you said you had commitments.'

'I don't want to rush away till I've had a chance to get to know Nick.'

Freya regarded him thoughtfully. 'But you do know it will be a week or more before we get the results?'

'A week, Freya? What's a week when you've had Nick for more than eleven years? Don't you understand that I need a chance to get to know my son?'

'Yes, of course I understand that. I'm sorry.' She looked as if she might weep.

'They're giving Nick's case priority,' he said in a more conciliatory tone. 'So we might hear quite soon.'

'That's good news, at least.'

Gus glanced at his wristwatch. 'It won't be too long before school's out and I thought Nick might like to come swimming with me this afternoon.'

'Oh?'

'I won't keep him too long. I know he has home-work.' He frowned at Freya. 'Nick does swim, doesn't he?'

'Of course. He's like me. He loves the water.'

Out of nowhere, something about the soft,

vulnerable droop of her lower lip triggered a memory for Gus. Damn it. He was recalling a folk song he'd heard years ago, a song about a forsaken mermaid.

He'd only heard it a couple of times—once at an outdoor folk festival and once on the radio—but each time the lament about a lost and heartsick mermaid had drenched him with memories of Freya.

For days afterwards, the memories had haunted him. He'd only shaken them off, eventually, by convincing himself that Freya Jones had moved on with her life just as he had. But how could he have guessed that she hadn't settled down with some lucky man? How could he have dreamed there was a child, a living connection that would link him to her for ever?

Perhaps it was because of the memory that he said, 'Freya, you're welcome to come swimming with us, if you like.'

'I…I can't go. I've got a gallery to look after.'

Gus looked about him at the empty rooms and the walls filled with artwork. He lifted an eyebrow in a silent question.

'I know it doesn't look very busy at the moment,'

she said, reading his thoughts. 'But you never know who might drop in. I can't close on a whim.'

'Pity.' He let his gaze travel over the colourful walls. 'You have some great paintings here.'

'Yes, I've been lucky.' Freya moved into the centre of the room, looking about her with evident satisfaction. 'I've managed to capture quite a bit of interest in this little gallery. It's developed a reputation and people are starting to come here from all over Australia. Now I have top artists asking me if they can hang their work here. It used to be the other way round.'

'That's quite an achievement,' Gus said, genuinely impressed.

She nodded, smiling, unable to hide her satisfaction.

'So are any of these paintings yours?'

'Yes.' Freya lifted a hand, about to point out her work.

'Hang on,' Gus said. 'Let's see if I can find yours.' After finding Nick in a tribe of similarly dressed footballers, he was feeling a tad smug.

Now, with vague memories of the sketches that Freya had drawn twelve years ago, Gus began to wander the rooms checking out the landscapes, seascapes, vibrant arrangements of tropical flowers and fruit, portraits, abstracts...

Freya stood watching him with her lips curled in a small smile and her eyes sparkling with an *I dare you* gleam.

It wasn't long before Gus was forced to admit defeat. He sent her an apologetic grin. 'I give up. These all look really good to me, but none of them screams *you.*' He made a circling gesture to the paintings all around him. 'I have to say, if you've painted any of these, you've improved a hell of a lot since high school.'

'I should jolly well hope so.' Smiling archly, she came and stood beside him, arms folded over her front. 'Just out of interest, which paintings do you like? Which ones appeal to you most?'

He must have looked anxious because Freya laughed. 'This isn't a trick question, Gus. I'm not going to slash my wrists if you don't pick mine. I'm just curious.'

'I'm no expert.'

'I know that.'

His gaze flickered over the fruit and flowers, paused briefly on a bright, daring landscape with

sand and palm trees, then on to a realistic sea-
scape with waves crashing onto rocks. He stopped
at a piece that seemed to be a collage of watercolours and paper of varying textures. It was
beautiful and incredibly clever—the sort of thing
he would buy for a woman, the sort of thing he
should have bought for Monique, perhaps.

He moved onto an abstract with stripes in
browns and ochres overlaid with splashes of char-
coal and crimson. 'If I was buying something
for myself, I would probably choose this one,' he
said, pointing.

Freya nodded. 'That's a Carl Barrow.' She
smiled. 'You have good taste. It's probably the
most expensive painting here.'

'Really?' He pointed to the collage. 'What
about that one? It's beautiful.'

'That's one of mine,' she said, turning pink.

'Wow.' Genuinely excited, he moved closer. 'I
really like the way you've grouped everything
and the combination of colours. It's incredibly
pleasing to the eye. Intricate without being clut-
tered.' He turned to her, beaming. 'Floss, you're
brilliant.'

'Well, thank you, sir.'

She was blushing prettily and her eyes were glowing with pleasure and he wanted to kiss her so badly he couldn't breathe.

Instead, he found himself saying, 'Why *don't* you come with us to the beach? Couldn't you put one of those signs on the door? *Closing early today. Sorry for the inconvenience.*'

Pink-cheeked, she pursed her lips as she considered this. Gus watched the slow blaze of concentration in her eyes as she weighed up the pros and cons. He had a fair idea that her curiosity about his fledgling bond with Nick would win out.

'I guess I could close up for an hour,' she said.

Gus grinned.

Freya smiled back at him. Their gazes held and, without warning, the flame of their old attraction burned brightly.

'Hey, Mum.'

Nick's voice startled them. He was standing at the door, hair awry, school bag dangling from one shoulder.

'Oh, Nick, that's good timing.' Freya's voice was strangely high-pitched and the colour in her cheeks deepened. 'Gus was just asking if you'd like to go for a swim.'

'Would I ever?' Nick's face was instantly alight. 'Thanks, Gus. Hey, what about you, Mum? Are you coming too?'

'Yes. I thought I might as well.'

'Awesome.'

This is so not wise, Freya told herself as she thrust her feet through appropriate holes and wriggled into her swimming costume. Closing the gallery for a swim with Gus on a Monday afternoon was quite possibly the dumbest thing she'd ever done.

She knew jolly well that she should have left Gus and Nick to go swimming alone, but she'd let two things sway her and neither of them were admirable. First—she was jealous of the newly developing relationship between her son and his father. She didn't want to feel left out.

Second—those few minutes alone with Gus in the gallery had been over-the-moon wonderful and, even though she knew such moments were as fragile as soap bubbles and could only lead to heartbreak, she wanted more.

She was a fool.

She sank onto the edge of her bed. She had to think this through before she made a serious mistake.

Surely she wasn't really so selfish that she was jealous of any time Gus spent with Nick? Not after she'd had the boy to herself for eleven and a half years? No, she might feel a tad worried that Gus could somehow steal Nick from her, but if that had been her only concern, she wouldn't have closed the gallery to play hooky at the beach.

The true cause of her foolishness was the other reason—the intoxicating glow she'd felt when Gus praised her painting. It was the *zing* in her veins when he looked into her eyes and the scary knowledge that she'd never stopped loving him, that she would steal any time to be with him, no matter how brief or unwise.

But, the trouble was, trying to recapture those moments was *very* unwise. A few moments could never add up to a lifetime, and it was a lifetime with Gus that Freya wanted. Why couldn't she remember that her lifestyle and Gus's were worlds apart?

When he'd chosen a wife, he'd chosen a woman

who was as different from her as it was possible to be.

Why couldn't she remember that Gus was here to help Nick and for no other reason?

'Mum!' Nick stuck his head around Freya's bedroom door. His face was smeared with white sunscreen and he was dressed in bathers. A beach towel was draped around his neck. 'Are you ready? Gus is back and he's waiting.'

'Almost ready. Give me a minute.'

Freya jumped up and butterflies danced in her stomach as she checked her swimsuit in the mirror. The last time Gus had seen her in bathers she'd been a girl in a bikini. What would he think of her now?

She'd chosen her favourite bathers in a pale yellow Hawaiian print because they gave her skin a rather nice glow. But were they too revealing? Did her backside look too big?

'Mum?' Nick called again from the hallway.

She would have to do. She grabbed a long beach shirt and slipped it on, pushed her feet into flip-flops. Out into the hall, she collected her hat and beach bag.

Nick was skipping ahead of her with excited glee.

Through the front window, Freya could see Gus waiting on the footpath and her heart skipped too, although she was more nervous than gleeful.

'This is so cool,' Nick sang. 'I'm going to the beach with my mother *and* my father.'

Oh, help.

'Nick,' Freya called.

The boy turned, read the caution in her face and looked instantly worried. 'What's the matter?'

'You mustn't get your hopes up. You…you can't expect…'

'What?' the boy demanded, frowning.

Freya looked at Nick's shining eyes. She saw her beautiful, clever, courageous half-man, and her heart shuddered as she thought of the terrible shadow that hung over him. Given everything he faced, it was cruel to let him hope for the impossible.

'I'm talking about Gus and…and me. We're not…um…we won't…' She groaned, angry at her clumsiness. 'Your father is here to help you, darling, to make sure you get well. But you mustn't hope that he and I will get back together.'

Right now, Nick was too excited to let any-thing bother him. He simply grinned and said, 'Whatever. Hurry up.'

Should she have spelled it out even more clearly? 'Nick!'

He turned back, eyes shining and Freya hadn't the heart to spoil his fun.

'Just remember, don't swim out too far,' she said.

'Aw, M-u-u-m.'

As they left their towels and jogged across the warm sand to the sea, Gus felt a need to suck in his abs. He was a long way from tubby, but he wasn't quite as streamlined as he'd been at eighteen, and for the first time in a long time it mattered.

The surf was magic. He'd forgotten the sheer exhilaration of catching a wave, of feeling it pick him up and rush headlong with him, carrying him forward with magnificent force, then dumping him in the foaming shallows, chest scraping on sand.

And he hadn't dreamed that this primitive pleasure would be so greatly enhanced by the company of a child. Nick was at his side the whole time, sometimes acting like a little kid, laughing and squealing, reaching for Gus's hand, even jumping onto his back as they dived through a wave.

At other times he was fiercely independent, catching waves fearlessly. Showing off.

The surf was a little rough and Gus felt a need to keep an eye on the boy the whole time and, truth be told, he was grateful for the distraction. If he hadn't been watching Nick, he would have been constantly staring at Freya in her stunning lemon and white swimsuit. He would have been mesmerised by her glistening and smooth wet skin and her long mermaid's hair, sleek against the curve of her neck and shoulders.

Actually, he wouldn't have simply been staring; he probably would have found a need to be close to her, finding excuses to touch.

But Freya was wiser than he was. She kept her distance. When the strap of her bathers slipped, she pulled it up a lot faster than she would have when she was younger, and there were no flirtatious smiles.

So it was a good thing that Nick was there,

always jumping between them, shrieking with glee and distracting Gus's attention, and preventing him from doing anything foolish. And, when the boy finally admitted he'd had enough of surfing, they went back to their beach towels, dripping and exhausted, and Poppy Jones provided a new distraction.

She was waiting for them, sitting on the sand beside their towels, looking as unconventionally glamorous as she always had in a colourful kaftan and with her long silver hair in a loopy chignon.

It was Nick who made the introductions.

'Hey, Poppy, guess what? My dad's here.'

'So I see.' Poppy smiled warmly at Freya and her grandson and a tad uncertainly at Gus.

Hello, here we go... Gus thought, drawing a sharp breath. Poppy had been no fan of his when he was young and he had no idea how she would receive him now. He wasn't even sure how big a role she'd played in Freya's decision to keep her pregnancy a secret.

One thing was certain; Gus would have preferred to be wearing more clothing when he met Freya's mother after such a long time. It was hard to feel dignified when he was half naked and dripping wet, especially when he was uncomfortably aware that this woman viewed him as the son of snobs and totally unsuitable for her daughter.

He manufactured a smile. 'How do you do, Poppy?'

'I'm very well, thanks, Gus.' Hopping nimbly to her feet, Poppy scooped up Nick's beach towel and wrapped him in it, giving him a fond hug as she did so.

To Gus's surprise, the boy didn't seem to mind his grandmother's public display of affection.

'Gus has spent the whole day at the hospital,' Freya told her mother.

Without releasing her embrace, Poppy turned to Gus. 'Freya tells me you've come back to help our boy.'

'Fingers crossed,' Gus said, nodding.

This time Poppy's smile was definitely warm. 'That's wonderful news. We're very grateful.' As she began to towel Nick's hair dry she said, 'Freya and Nick always come to my place for dinner on Monday nights. Would you like to join us tonight, Gus?'

'Yes!' Nick punched the air with a triumphant fist.

Gus sensed rather than saw the way Freya stiffened.

'Easy there, Nick,' she said in a gently warning tone. 'Remember what I said. Gus might have other plans.'

Freya flashed a significant glance Gus's way and he knew she was giving him the perfect opening to bow out. He wondered if she was worried that this could be an awkward evening and he thought fast, trying to decide what was best.

'I have a curry simmering away,' Poppy told him. 'There's plenty for everyone.'

Never once in the time he'd gone out with Freya had Poppy offered him a meal, but now, with her grandson's life hanging in the balance, that barrier appeared to be finally down.

Gus couldn't help feeling pleased, but hadn't he planned to keep an emotional distance? Dining with this trio would be rather like playing Happy Families, and it might confuse Nick. Even so, Gus wanted to accept. He'd been an outsider for too long.

Three pairs of eyes were watching him, waiting

for his answer. Poppy was looking mildly amused, Freya was as tense as an athlete waiting for the starter's gun, and Nick looked full of hope.

It was the hope in Nick's eyes that decided Gus. After all, the boy was the reason he was here. 'Thanks, Poppy,' he said. 'I'd love to join you, but I need to duck back to the hotel to change.'

Nick began to dance a little jig of excitement.

'We have to change, too,' Freya said and she seemed surprisingly relieved. 'And Nick has to do his homework.'

Poppy gave them all a pleased smile. 'Dinner will be ready at seven.'

Dining in Poppy's warm, cosy kitchen *did* feel like Happy Families. Dangerously so. Despite the super-neat sparkling white exterior, the inside of her cottage was as exotic and colourful as her clothing, and when Gus was welcomed at the front door by Nick, he was also met by the smells of jasmine-scented candles mingled with the fragrant aroma of curry.

Nick's eyes popped wide when he saw the wine and flowers Gus carried. 'Are they for my mum?'

Gus winced inwardly when he saw the boy's delight. 'Actually, they're for your grandmother. Poppy's the hostess,' Gus explained. 'She's gone to all the trouble of cooking a meal for us.'

The boy shrugged and pulled a face as if he'd never understand grown-ups, then led Gus down a pea-green hallway to the kitchen.

Gus's eyes were drawn immediately to Freya, who was setting the table. She'd fixed her hair into a high twist and had threaded gold hoops in her ears, and she was wearing jeans with a top made from something soft and floaty in muted browns, beiges and pinks. When she saw Gus she smiled and he came to a heart-thudding standstill.

Her smile seemed to glow, as if she was lit from within, and heaven knew how long he might have stood there, drinking in the sight of her, if Nick hadn't piped up.

'Poppy, Gus has brought you presents.'

Coming to his senses, Gus handed the gifts to Poppy, who blushed like a girl and gave him an unexpected hug. 'I can't remember the last time a man brought me flowers.'

'What a lovely thought, Gus,' Freya said and she smiled so warmly, he kissed her on the cheek.

The kiss felt more significant than it should have.

Poppy was animated as she deftly arranged the flowers in a vase and set them on a brilliant pink dresser. 'Freya, find us some glasses, dear. Do we need a corkscrew? It's in the drawer next to the sink. Can you deal with that, Gus? Oh, and there's lemonade in the fridge for you, Nick. Help yourself, darling.'

For a few moments there was general fuss as drinks were organised and steaming pots of rice and curry were set on mats in the centre of the table. The hubbub died as everyone sat down. A gentle breeze drifted in through the kitchen window along with the sounds of waves breaking. *Thump, crump, swish.* Poppy's house was right on the edge of the sand, as close to the sea as it was possible to be.

'I'd forgotten what it's like to live so near to the sea that you can hear it all the time,' Gus said.

'I don't know if I could live without it now,' said Poppy. 'It's almost like having another heartbeat.'

'And when I sleep over at Poppy's the waves sing me to sleep,' Nick chimed in happily.

Yes… Gus could remember all too clearly a night when he'd slept here with Freya, close to the singing of the waves. Had there ever been a more perfect night?

He wondered about the times Nick stayed at his grandmother's. Where was Freya on those occasions? Out on dates? He discovered this wasn't a question he wanted to dwell on.

'This smell of curry reminds me of Africa,' he said.

Of course they plied him with questions then and, as Poppy dished up spoonfuls of rice and fragrant meat, he told them about Eritrea in the horn of Africa.

'Where's the horn of Africa?' demanded Nick.

'Go and get the globe from the lounge room and Gus can show you,' Poppy told him.

Nick was back in a moment, bearing a large old-fashioned globe, which he handed to Gus. Then he stood leaning against the back of Gus's chair with a hand resting casually on his shoulder, his breath soft and warm on the back of Gus's neck.

'The names of the countries have changed since

this globe was made,' Gus told him. 'But here's Eritrea, next to Ethiopia.' He traced Eritrea's borders. 'And here's the Red Sea, which forms another part of its border.'

'Isn't Asmara the capital?' asked Freya.

'That's right.'

As Nick went back to his place and they started to eat, Gus told them about Asmara's beautiful Italian colonial architecture, and about the islands and reefs in the Red Sea and the desolate magnetism of the wastelands of Dankalia in the south.

'Did you see lots of elephants?' Nick asked.

Gus shook his head. 'I'm afraid I didn't see many at all. There are only about a hundred elephants left in Eritrea.'

'What's happened to them?'

'Most of them were killed in the war.'

Nick looked horrified. 'Which war?'

'A long, long war with Ethiopia. The people in Eritrea were struggling for independence and it went on for years and years. It was a very hard time for the people and the animals. There were droughts as well as war, and lots of sickness.'

Gus looked from Freya to Poppy. 'Sorry, this

isn't exactly a pleasant subject to discuss over
dinner.'

Freya smiled. 'We're used to it. These aren't the
worst questions Nick's asked at dinner time.' To
Nick she said, 'It's because of the wars and the
drought that Gus went to work in Africa, to help
the Eritreans.'

Nick was wide-eyed, clearly impressed. 'How
did you help them?'

'Mainly by working alongside them. My job
was to help them to fight the drought, so I was
involved in sinking wells and building dams
and finding drought-resistant crops for them to
grow.'

'What about your wife? Was she helping them,
too?'

Across the table, Freya's eyes met Gus's in a
direct, cool challenge, and it took him a second
or two to respond.

'Monique taught in one of the hospital medical schools,' he said. 'And she worked to educate
people generally about health care.'

Nick's eyes were huge. 'How did she die?'

'*Nick!*' There was both a warning and an edge
of panic in Freya's voice.

CHAPTER SEVEN

Gus managed a shaky smile. He knew Freya was upset, but he didn't want to reprimand Nick. The boy was bright and almost certainly understood that his hold on life was at risk. Chances were the whole question of death plagued him much more than he let on.

It was even possible that an honest answer would help Nick.

Even so, talking about the way Monique died always brought a sickening chill that soaked Gus to the bone. At least he was used to the feeling now. After two years, he knew it would come whenever he spoke about this.

'My wife was killed in an explosion,' he told them. 'She took a wrong turn and she drove her truck over a landmine left behind from the war.'

'Oh, God,' Poppy whispered.

'I'm so sorry,' said Freya, white-lipped.

An uncomfortable silence fell over the table and, rather than allow it to go on for too long, Gus felt a need to resurrect the mood. 'Wars are terrible things, but the Eritreans are getting on with their lives now. Freya, have you seen any of the contemporary art coming out of Africa? I think you'd love it.'

Freya brightened visibly. 'Actually, I've been lucky enough to see an exhibition in Canberra. I thought it was amazing. So much energy and excitement in the work. I especially loved the sculptures.'

She went on to tell Gus about the artists she particularly admired and, to the adults' relief, Nick found this topic boring and he stopped asking questions.

He saved them for much later…when they were home again and Freya had tucked him in and kissed him goodnight and was turning out his bedroom light.

'Mum?' the boy called through the darkness. 'Do you like Gus?'

The question zapped through poor Freya as if she'd been spiked by an electric probe. Her legs threatened to give way and she clutched at the door frame for balance. 'Of course I like him.'

'I mean *really* like him.'

Oh, help. She thought she'd nipped this in the bud. Tonight, however, after they'd washed up Poppy's dishes together, Gus had walked home with them and Nick had walked between them, talking animatedly the whole way, skipping at times, even linking arms with them in moments of pure elation. When they'd said goodnight to Gus at the front gate, the boy had given him a bear hug and clung to him for dear life.

Remembering the poignancy of that moment now, Freya felt tears prick the backs of her eyelids. Her knees were distinctly wobbly as she walked back to Nick's bed and sat on the edge of the mattress.

'Nick, you haven't forgotten what I told you, have you? You know Gus and I won't be getting back together.'

'But that's crazy. Why won't you?'

Freya sighed. 'You know Gus hasn't come here to see me. He's only here because of you.'

'But he wants to see you, too. He's always looking at you. I reckon he likes you.'

He's always looking at you. Freya pushed aside
the silly little thrill these words caused. 'Well,
yes…Gus likes me as an old friend, but that's
all. Darling, you have to understand it doesn't
mean we're going to…er…start living together
or anything like that.'

Moonlight shining through the blinds above
Nick's bed illuminated the pout of Nick's lower
lip, and then the glitter of tears in his eyes.

Freya hugged him. 'Nicky boy.' It was an en-
dearment from his baby days. 'Don't be sad, darling. Now that Gus knows about you, he's going
to want to stay in touch with you always. I'm sure
you'll see lots of him. He's so proud of you.'

'But what if he just disappears again?'

'He won't, Nick.'

'Grandpa did.'

'Oh, darling.' Freya gave him a hug. 'I told
you Gus is a very different man from Grandpa.
Everything about this situation is different. Gus
is thrilled that you're his son. I know how much
you mean to him already.'

She stroked Nick's hair away from his forehead.
It had the habit of falling forward the same way
Gus's did. 'Now he's met you and knows how

fantastic you are, there's no way he'd want to lose contact.'

Using a corner of his sheet, Nick swiped at his eyes. 'I suppose if Gus gives me his kidney, he'll have to come back to make sure I'm looking after it properly.'

'You bet he will.' Somehow, Freya held back the emotion that threatened to choke her. She was so aware of how the boy picked up on the smallest unconscious messages, positive or negative.

Now she forced herself to picture Nick healthy and strong, spending precious times with his dad long into the future. 'And that will be perfect, won't it?' she said.

Everything would be perfect, she told herself as she left the room, once Nick was well and happy.

But how would she cope with Gus dropping in and out of their lives? It would be so much easier if she wasn't still hopelessly in love with him.

Waiting to hear back about the tests was a new form of torture for Gus. He tried to keep busy, staying in touch with the project in the Northern Territory via phone calls and email, and he used his hire car to tour the district, rediscovering for-gotten haunts. He saw Nick when he could in the afternoons after school and they went swimming or for runs on the beach with Urchin.

Freya emailed an entire photo album devoted to Nick and he pored over these snaps, fascinated by the gradual transformation of his son from tiny baby to chubby toddler to small child, then schoolboy. Sometimes he caught glimpses of Freya's smile, or he saw an expression in Nick's eyes that reminded him of himself as a child. But mostly Nick was his own unique self, his features becoming more clearly defined as he grew.

To Gus's surprise, he discovered that he no longer felt the same raging disappointment for the lost years when he hadn't known his son. He knew Nick now and that seemed to matter more.

The past was gone and, for all he knew, he might have stuffed up being a father. But he and Nick still had the present. And, heaven help him, if he was a perfect match and if the surgeons did their job well, Nick could look forward to a long and healthy life, and Gus planned to be involved.

Right now, with his heart melting over these glimpses into his son's life, Gus knew without question that, even if he lived on the other side of the globe, even if his relationship with the boy's mother remained fragile, he would make sure he was a part of Nick's future.

More than once Gus considered inviting Freya to join him for lunch at the hotel. Despite his lingering sense of injustice, he wanted to get to know her better, for all kinds of reasons, and her intimate knowledge of Nick was only one of them. There was a quiet self-assurance about Freya now that intrigued him, and a mysterious allure—sadness and shyness mixed with beauty and courage.

She'd changed in many ways and Gus wanted to understand how and why.

But he didn't invite her. She'd made it clear that she didn't want to get too pally with him, and she was sensible to be wary. Nick was her focus and the boy needed every ounce of her attention and love. The very last thing she needed right now was the distraction of an old boyfriend.

Just the same, Gus couldn't believe how hard it was to keep his distance from Freya. To start with, he saw her every day and each day she seemed to grow more beautiful. She was still like a Siren and being back in the Bay, surrounded by the sights and sounds and smells that accompanied their long-ago romance, was almost more trying than waiting for the test results.

Gus found himself recalling every detail of falling in love with her.

It had been so amazing to discover at the end of high school that the shy, elusive girl he'd been lusting after for two years was as interested in him as he was in her. At first it had felt like a miracle but, as the weeks of that summer rolled on, and in spite of their parents' misgivings, he and Freya had grown closer and closer.

They would walk for miles along the coast just to be completely alone. The first time they made love, they were in a tiny secluded cove that was a two-hour hike from Sugar Bay.

Thinking about it now, Gus could still remember the heady scent of the sun on Freya's skin and the silky smoothness of her tanned limbs, could remember her eagerness, her sweetness, her boldness.

And she hadn't minded his fumbling nervousness.

He'd made love with more assurance and finesse the next time…on a stolen weekend in Poppy's house…

Poppy hardly ever left the Bay, but she'd been invited to a birthday party for a friend who lived in Gympie and she was away for the entire weekend.

Freya had rung Gus at home. 'Guess what? We have the house to ourselves for a whole weekend.'

'Damn.'

'Damn?'

'I'm supposed to be giving Mel a hand on the petrol pump this afternoon.'

'Can't you get out of it? Swap with someone?'

He'd tried to con several mates into taking his place at the garage and he'd eventually bribed Fred Bartlet, promising to let Fred use his surfboard every day for a fortnight.

When he arrived at Freya's, she greeted him at the front door wearing nothing but a smile and a pink sarong, and she'd lit scented candles and decorated her bed with a lavender tie-dyed sheet and frangipani petals.

They made love. They went for swims, came home and showered and made love again. They were sweet and tender. They were wicked and wild. They kissed and touched in ways they'd only read about or heard about, and they almost cried with the beauty and out-and-out fabulousness of it all.

They talked long into the night and cooked up a midnight feast, and Gus discovered that a girl like Freya could be so much more than a lover— she could also be his best friend.

Hell.

How had he ever forgotten that? How had he let her slip away? Had he been under a spell that had broken the minute he left the Bay?

One thing was certain. It was too late to go back to the golden age of eighteen and he would drive himself mad if he kept asking these questions now.

After three restless days, Gus poked his head in at the Crane Brothers' garage, where he found Mel in the middle of rebuilding an engine.

Mel lifted his cheery grease-smeared face from

beneath the bonnet of a cream Citroën. 'Sorry, mate, can't stop. Old Bill Nixon wants this running smoothly for his granddaughter's wedding on Saturday. Won't get away till this evening. But how about we sink a cold one at the pub, say around half past six?'

Early evening found the two old friends perched on high stools at a bar overlooking the bay, reminiscing about their youth as they munched on salted peanuts and drank beer from tall frosty glasses. Mel had always been a great story-teller and Gus enjoyed hearing what their old friends were up to these days, as well as receiving proud updates about Mel's wife Shelley and their two children, a boy and a girl.

But eventually, inevitably perhaps, the conversation swung around to Freya and Nick.

Gus came back from the bar with their second round of drinks and set them down, and Mel said without preamble, 'That boy of Freya's is a fabulous kid, Gus.'

Despite the skip in Gus's heartbeats, he nodded carefully and sampled his beer.

'And I'm not just talking about his football skills,' said Mel. 'Nick's been amazing, the way he's handled this whole business with his kidneys. He never whinges or talks about it. Just gets on with his life.'

Emotion tied painful knots in Gus's throat and he was suddenly unable to speak.

Mel eyed him shrewdly. 'Shut me up if I'm speaking out of turn, mate, but I reckon maybe Nick's a chip off the old block.'

Something inside Gus struck hard, as if his heart had sounded a gong. 'Which old block would that be, Mel?'

Momentarily, Mel was taken aback, but he recovered quickly and shrugged. 'The one sitting right in front of me, perhaps?'

There was no point in trying to deny the truth. Gus let out his breath slowly. 'I suppose the whole Bay knows by now?'

'Well, maybe not the *whole* Bay.' Mel sent him a cautiously crooked smile. 'Three-quarters maybe, but not *everyone*.'

'Which means that almost the entire population of Sugar Bay found out I'm Nick's father just a day or two after I did.' Gus scowled as the anger and hurt he'd almost laid to rest blasted back with a vengeance.

'You were in the dark? You're joking.' Mel grimaced uncomfortably. He took a swig of beer. 'That's rough.' Then another swig. When he set the glass down, he regarded Gus thoughtfully. 'You mean to say Freya never told you she was pregnant?'

'I had no idea,' Gus said coldly. Damn it, he thought he'd come to grips with the years of secrecy, but talking about it to Mel ripped the wound wide open.

Mel shook his head. 'That's a shocker. At the end of high school we all thought you and Freya were the couple most likely to—'

'Likely to what?'

Mel grimaced. 'I don't know—get together and stay together, I guess.'

Gus gritted his teeth so fiercely he was surprised they didn't crack. He knew it was true. Back in that summer between the end of high school and leaving Sugar Bay, he and Freya had been infatuated with each other, inseparable.

Looking back, he found it almost impossible to pinpoint how and when he'd changed, but it must have started almost as soon as he left for

Brisbane. How else, after six short weeks, had he
been able to let her go so easily?

Eighteen was such an impressionable, fickle
age.

But was that an excuse?

The worst of it was that he'd changed so fast
and so radically he'd frightened Freya off. But he
wasn't about to confess to Mel Crane that she'd
actually tried to tell him about their baby.

'I know it's not really any of my business,'
Mel said, watching Gus carefully. 'But, for what
it's worth, no one around here knew who Nick's
father was. One or two thought it might have been
you, but Freya and Poppy went away up north
for a few months. Freya was pregnant when she
came back, and she was very close-lipped about
the circumstances.'

'I guess Poppy took her away to muddy the
waters,' Gus said moodily.

'I guess.' Mel thought about this for a bit, then
brightened. 'I can tell you one thing, Gus—Freya's
done a great job with that boy. A fantastic job.'
Mel shrugged. 'As a footie coach, I've seen every
kind of family. In my teams there are kids with
no mum, no dad, parents who never turn up to

watch their kids play, other parents who scream at their kids and yell abuse at the ref.'

Mel eyed Gus steadily over the rim of his glass. 'There's no argument. You would have been a huge bonus in Nick's life. But, putting that aside, the simple fact is Freya's done a great job. Heck, she let the boy play a game she doesn't even like, and I really respect that. I'm sure she'd rather he played tennis.'

Gus smiled in wry acknowledgement of this.

'Shelley really likes Freya,' Mel went on. 'So do her married friends, and that's saying something. I've seen other good-looking single women who bring out the claws of the married ones, but everyone here likes Freya.'

Still staring moodily into his drink, Gus said, 'What surprises me is that she hasn't married.'

'Too right. And it's not for lack of opportunity. Nearly every bachelor in the district has set his cap at her.'

Mel started to chuckle, then seemed to think better of it. His face sobered. 'So, mate, what's the story with Nick? Is he going to be OK?'

'That's the plan. I'm certainly hoping he'll be absolutely fine.'

'With the help of a kidney from you?'

'Yeah. We're still waiting to hear if I'm a suitable match.' As Gus said that, his mobile phone began to buzz in his pocket. 'Excuse me.' His chest tightened as he retrieved it and saw the number. 'Bit of a coincidence. This is from the renal physician's office. I'll take it outside.'

Gus's heartbeats were thundering as he hurried quickly from the bar. 'Hello?'

'Mr Wilder? I have a message from Dr Kingston.'

Thud. 'Yes?'

'He has the results back from the blood and tissue cross-matching, and he'd like you to make an appointment to see him.'

'Yes, sure. When?'

'As soon as possible. Is there any chance you could be in Brisbane by tomorrow morning?'

'Absolutely.'

'Great. We can fit you in at eleven.'

A week later, Gus made the journey to Brisbane again, this time with Freya and Nick. During the entire trip down the highway Freya's stomach churned as she swung through a spectrum of emotions from hope and excitement to fear and abject terror.

The past week had been such a whirlwind of preparations ever since they heard that Gus was a perfect match for Nick. His blood type, his tissue samples, the state of his kidneys, his heart, his lungs and his mind made him a perfect live donor. If everything went well, Nick could live to a healthy old age.

But if it didn't…

Freya couldn't bear to think of failure, couldn't let her imagination go there. And yet, no amount of level-headedness could hold off the knife-edge of panic.

Now she wasn't only worried about Nick. She was worried about Gus, too. The procedure should be straightforward but in any operation there was always a risk.

Two people she loved were facing possible danger…

'Don't look so glum,' Gus told her when they stopped for a cuppa at a roadside café.

'Sorry.' For Nick's sake, she knew she had to be totally optimistic and excited.

As they stood at the counter placing their

orders—tea, a long black and a strawberry milkshake—Gus leaned close and whispered in Freya's ear, 'It's going to be OK.'

She looked up, saw the warmth and confidence in his eyes and her heart took wings. When Gus pressed a warm kiss on her cheek, she longed to let her eyes drift closed and to lean into his strength.

Perhaps if Nick hadn't been watching them so closely she might have done exactly that.

In Brisbane they stayed in adjacent suites in a hotel close to the hospital. Gus insisted on paying for their accommodation and he wouldn't listen to Freya's protests. 'So far, I haven't contributed a cent to Nick's upkeep,' he said.

Their appointment with Dr Lee, the transplant coordinator, was for three o'clock. As they sat in the waiting room, Nick read a comic that Freya had bought him—one of his favourite space adventures—while she flicked through a celebrity gossip magazine without seeing anything on the pages.

Gus reached for her hand and gave it an encouraging squeeze and she answered with a brave smile. His touch had the power to make her feel hopeful and she would have liked to keep holding his hand.

At last they went inside. Dr Lee greeted them warmly, then took them through what would happen over the next few days. Tomorrow, they were to arrive at the hospital early for a final day-long evaluation of Nick that would include more blood tests and an ECG. The medical team would do a final cross-match to make sure Nick could still receive Gus's kidney. And Nick would begin taking drugs to prevent his body from rejecting the new kidney.

The doctor took them calmly through every step of the procedures, making the transplant sound very routine and unthreatening. Freya stole glances at Gus and Nick, caught them exchanging fond, almost excited smiles, and her heart filled to overflowing with love for both of them, and with pride and admiration, too. They were both so strong. They were her heroes. For their sakes, she resolved to remain calm and optimistic.

It was, after all, the only way to get through the next few days.

* * *

After the journey and the appointments and a meal at Nick's favourite pasta and pizza place, the boy was ready for bed quite early. Neither Freya nor Gus was sleepy though, so they sat on the balcony outside Freya's hotel suite, looking at the city lights and talking.

Mostly they talked about Nick.

Freya filled in details, giving Gus a potted history of their son's milestones—when he'd crawled and learned to walk, and how he'd skinned his knee trying to fly off Poppy's top step. She told him about the time, when Nick was three, that he'd wandered away from home, and how terrified she'd been until she'd found him at the shop around the corner.

'He'd found ten cents and he was trying to buy fish food,' she said, smiling at the memory. 'He wanted to feed the little fish he'd seen swimming in the shallows.'

They both chuckled over that, and it was all kinds of wonderful for Freya to sit with Gus while their son slept in a room nearby. She could almost pretend they'd been doing this for years. And what a seductive picture that was—to imagine that she and Gus were conventional parents, happily living under one roof, an intact family.

For a reckless moment she let her mind elaborate on the fantasy. She saw herself sharing meals with Gus, saw them curled on a sofa enjoying glasses of wine, sharing the same bed.

Oh, God. She was sure her face was glowing bright red. What a fool she was.

But she was so happy for Nick that his father had come into his life. The man was handsome and friendly and thoughtful and generally wonderful. Over and above that, he was making a huge sacrifice. It was no wonder the boy adored and worshipped him.

If only…

No…it was pointless to wish she'd made different decisions in the past. They had felt right at the time and it was a useless exercise to keep going back over them and wondering…

'Nick talked to me about your father,' Gus said, suddenly breaking into Freya's thoughts. 'You're right. That old con man has shaken the boy's faith.'

'That was such a terrible Christmas.' She shook her head, remembering. 'Poor Nick. He was singing in the Nippers' choir at Carols by Candlelight and he thought his grandfather was out in the crowd, watching and listening. But that was actually when Sean took off. During the carols. It was such a dirty trick.'

'He's still worried I'm going to disappear, too.'

'I've tried to reassure him.'

'So have I. I told him I have to go back to the Northern Territory once this is over, but I plan to keep seeing him on a regular basis. I mean it, Freya. I'll stay in touch. And I'll come back as often as I can.'

Her soft whoosh of relief was barely audible, thank heavens. She knew there was no point in feeling too happy just because Gus promised to stay in touch. It was Nick he wanted to visit. He might even want to take Nick away with him from time to time and she would have to get used to waving them goodbye.

Those thoughts made her unnecessarily gloomy, so she forced herself to smile. 'Nick told me you'll have to keep coming back to make sure he's looking after your kidney properly.'

'Yeah.' Gus tried to laugh, but the sound was

strangled. He cleared his throat. 'He's such a brave little guy.' His face softened and he looked away into the distance, then let out a heavy sigh.

'Actually,' he said quietly, 'I took the opportunity to tell Nick that he has more than one grandfather.'

'Oh...well...yes.' Freya winced as her guilty conscience gave a nasty jab in her solar plexus. 'I'm sorry, Gus. I should have asked before. How *are* your parents?'

'They're both very well, thank you. They live in Perth these days. My sister moved over there when she married, and she has a baby now. Mum couldn't bear to be living on the opposite coast from her grandchild.'

For the first time in too long, Freya recalled Gus's conservative middle-class parents. When they'd lived in Sugar Bay, Gus's father had been the town's most influential and hard-nosed bank manager. He and his wife had never mixed with the hippie commune at the far end of the Bay.

Bill and Deirdre Wilder had always found it very hard to hide their disapproval of Freya but, to give them their due, they'd behaved no more coldly towards her than Poppy had towards Gus.

'Have you told your parents about Nick?'

Gus nodded. 'I rang them two days ago.'

'That must have been hard.'

'It wasn't the easiest phone call I've made.'

Freya looked down at her hands, tightly clenched in her lap. There was no condemnation in Gus's voice, but she couldn't help thinking that here were more people hurt by her secrecy. 'Were they shocked?'

'Of course. Shocked and concerned.' Shooting her a bright sideways glance, he said, 'They'd like to fly over here to see Nick.'

'That would be lovely.' She forced her hands to relax. 'So I take it they've recovered from their shock?'

'Yes, and with surprising speed. Mum rang straight back to assure me.'

Freya wasn't proud of the way her heart sank, but the thought of dealing with Gus's parents on top of everything else was rather daunting. She hunted for a nice safe direction to steer their conversation but, to her surprise, Gus frowned suddenly and his jaw jutted as if he was preparing to confront her.

A shiver skittered over her. Instinctively, she straightened her shoulders and lifted her chin. She almost demanded *What?* the way Nick did when he knew he was about to get into trouble.

Gus's eyes were a dark challenge. 'I have to say I'm very surprised that you haven't married.'

If he'd zapped her with a stun gun he couldn't have startled her more.

'M-married?' she repeated stupidly, while her heartbeats took off at a gallop.

'You're a lovely woman, Freya, and I know you've had plenty of admirers.'

'Who've you been talking to?'

'Mel.'

'Oh.' She tried to shrug this off. 'Mel could gossip for Australia.'

Gus didn't respond. He watched her with a moody frown as he leaned back in his chair, legs stretched casually in front of him, waiting for her to talk about the men in her life.

If any other man had asked Freya this, she would have told him what he could do with his nosy questions, but this was Gus, the father of her son. He wasn't asking about her boyfriends out of jealousy, or because he wanted to make a move on her. He probably wondered why she hadn't found a man to stand in as a male role model for Nick.

'Mel's right,' she said. 'There have been boyfriends. Mostly local fellows, who were good company.' She shrugged. 'A few years ago, I met a really nice guy from Melbourne through my work.' She stopped, unwilling to add that this man was interesting and intelligent, and he'd liked Nick, and he'd been keen to commit to something more permanent.

Gus frowned at her savagely. 'Go on. Why didn't it work out?'

Didn't he know? Couldn't he guess?

Freya's mouth curled in a sad smile as she shrugged elaborately. 'No sparks.'

'None?' Gus challenged, glaring fiercely.

'Not enough.' Not enough to commit to a long-term relationship. Freya had been scared that Jason's niceness would bore her eventually, but she wasn't going to tell Gus that.

Her face was burning, so she turned away and missed his reaction. He didn't speak and for long, uncomfortable moments they both sat very still, staring down at the ceaseless lines of traffic while she wondered about the women in *his* life—especially his wife.

Eventually, she couldn't help herself. If Gus could interrogate her, surely she could ask at least some of the questions that were keeping her awake at night.

'What about you, Gus? Can you tell me about Monique?' She saw the tightening in his facial muscles. 'Unless it's too painful to talk about.'

'It's OK,' he said gruffly. 'What would you like to know?'

Nothing. Everything…

'Oh, I don't know—how you met, perhaps?'

Gus shifted uncomfortably. 'It was all very straightforward. We met through our work. We were both in a remote village, the only non-Africans around, so we kind of drifted together, I guess.'

The way he told it, their relationship sounded more like a convenient friendship than a romance. But it must have been romantic. Freya had seen Gus in love and she knew how very passionate and tender he could be.

'Did you ever bring her back to Australia? Were you married here?'

'No, we were married in Africa. Our parents came over for the wedding.'

We were married. The words pierced Freya as if Gus had fired them from a blowgun.

The pain was so much worse than the familiar ache she usually felt when she thought about Gus Wilder and it proved to her, once and for all, that she was, unfortunately, still seriously hung up on him. Then she tortured herself further by picturing Gus as a bridegroom with his beautiful, happy bride on his arm.

She could imagine his delighted parents meeting Monique's delighted parents. *Don't they make a beautiful couple? And so worthy of each other.*

To ask more questions would be like pushing something sharp beneath her fingernails, but Freya couldn't leave the subject alone.

Was Monique beautiful? She mentally cancelled that and asked him instead, 'What did Monique look like?'

Gus frowned. The smallest smile flickered. 'Very French. Dark eyes. Straight black hair. French nose.'

'What does a French nose look like?'

He grinned. 'Oh, you know. Rather pointy.'

Freya could hear the fondness in his voice and she wished she didn't mind so very much. Of course Gus had loved his wife.

But a loud sigh escaped him and suddenly he slumped forward, elbows sunk on his knees.

'Gus, I'm sorry. I'm as bad as Nick, asking far too many awkward questions.'

'It's OK. It's not the questions…'

'But the memories must hurt…'

Gus lifted his head. 'Yes, they do, but perhaps not quite in the way you imagine.'

As Freya puzzled over this, he stood abruptly and went to the balcony's railing. For a moment or two he looked down into the lines of traffic below, and when he turned back to Freya his face was bleak. 'Actually, it's the guilt that bothers me more than anything.'

'Guilt?' Freya's heart lurched sickeningly. What on earth could he mean?

'Monique was ready to leave Eritrea,' Gus said. 'But I persuaded her to stay on for an extra six months, till I'd finished the dam project.'

And some time during those six months

Monique had driven over the landmine, Freya guessed. Her heart went out to him. 'Gus, you mustn't blame yourself.'

When he didn't respond, she said, 'But I think I understand. When something bad happens to someone you love, it's easy to convince yourself that you're somehow to blame.'

Frowning, Gus lifted his gaze to meet hers. 'You don't blame yourself for Nick's condition, do you?'

'It's easy to do. There are times when I beat myself up, thinking that maybe I did something wrong. Or there was something I didn't do that I should have. So many times I've wished I'd taken him to the doctor sooner...'

The bleakness left Gus's face and his eyes were suddenly unexpectedly tender. 'Freya, from what I've heard, you've been a fabulous mother. Perfect, in fact.'

She'd been far from perfect but, under the circumstances, it was generous of Gus to say so. 'I suppose I'm like most mothers. I do my best. You can only ever do your best.'

But she was sure Gus must have been wondering, as she often did, whether things might have been different if the two of them had raised Nick together.

The blast of a car horn reached them from the traffic below. Freya looked at her watch. 'I shouldn't be keeping you up too late,' she said. 'You need to be in tip-top condition for the final round of tests tomorrow.'

Apparently Gus agreed, for he left quite promptly. After he'd gone, Freya made herself a cup of hot chocolate using one of the sachets provided by the hotel and she drank it in bed, but she took ages to get to sleep.

It was so silly. After so many sleepless nights worrying about finding a match for Nick, that weight had been taken off her shoulders. She should have been relaxed, not tossing and turning, not questioning the decision she'd made all those years ago.

Thing was, until Gus had turned up, she was sure she'd made the right decision for both of them, but now…

The more she saw of Gus being wonderful and charming and sexy, the more she remembered how much she'd loved him. When she'd made that fateful journey to the university to see him she'd thought he was changing, but he hadn't changed at all. Not only was he as attractive and sexy as ever, he was warm and kind and thoughtful...

Freya groaned and buried her face in her pillow but she couldn't block out her memories. *Oh, help.* She could remember the comfort of Gus's embrace, and she could still taste his kisses. Could still feel the warm eagerness of his lips on hers, and the sensual heaven of his lips on her throat and her breasts.

She could remember kissing him all over, discovering the scents of the sea on his skin.

Oh, God. It was no good. She couldn't go on tormenting herself like this. She got up to make another cup of hot chocolate and to find something safely unromantic to read.

CHAPTER EIGHT

DR LEE strode into the waiting room, grinning and giving the thumbs-up signal. 'Good news. It's all systems go.'

The tests were completed and he'd come to report that the transplant would take place the very next day, beginning at nine o'clock in the morning and finishing some time around one in the afternoon.

Freya's stomach began to churn with a mixture of hope and fear.

With Dr Lee's blessing, she and Gus took Nick to a late afternoon matinee to watch a space adventure with a guaranteed feel good, happy ending. But then they had to go back to the hospital where he would stay overnight to start the anti-rejection medication.

Sitting in his hospital bed in brand-new pyjamas covered in rocket ships, Nick grinned at

Gus. 'By this time tomorrow I'll have your kidney inside me.'

'You're very welcome to it, mate.' Gus's voice was rough with emotion.

'No more global warning.' Nick grinned again, but Freya could see the fear lurking behind the bright smile and she felt impossibly weepy. Of course, she'd known for ages now that her boy was a super brave little guy, but his courage still got to her every time.

'I'll be here first thing, early in the morning,' she told him when he began to look sleepy.

'And you'll bring Gus, won't you?'

'Yes, darling, of course.'

As she hugged Nick, she willed herself to be braver. If he could get through this without a whimper, then she must, too.

Gus gave Nick a hug. 'I've checked out the nurses and I haven't seen any vampires, have you?'

Nick shook his head and giggled.

'But, just in case, I brought you a weapon.' Gus reached into his deep trouser pocket and produced a little string of garlic cloves.

Where on earth had he found them?

'These will keep the hungriest vampire at bay,'

he announced. 'They're in all the hospitals, you know. They try to look normal.'

Nick laughed. 'Thanks for the warning.' Eyes sparkling, he surveyed the sparsely furnished room. 'Where will I keep this? Under my pillow?'

'Garlic might be a bit smelly,' Freya suggested tentatively, worried that Nick might get into trouble, but not wanting to spoil their game.

'I'd say we should put in here,' Gus said, pulling out the drawer in the bedside table. 'Can you reach it?'

'Easy.' Nick demonstrated a quick snatch. 'Cool. I was wondering what I'd do if a vampire snuck in here in the middle of the night.'

'There will be nurses in and out all night,' Freya felt compelled to explain.

'Yeah, Mum, I know.'

Nick winked at Gus, and just for a moment, Freya felt on the outside, then she squashed the feeling. She really was delighted that her son and his dad were getting on so well.

For all sorts of reasons, Freya was glad of Gus's company as they tiptoed out of Nick's room and down the long hospital corridor. They'd waited till he dropped off to sleep, but she'd hated leaving him, even though he'd insisted he didn't need his mum and he wasn't a baby.

'You've got a big day tomorrow, too,' she told Gus as they reached the ground floor.

He turned to her with an easy smile. 'But we have to eat, and I'd like to take you out to dinner.'

'Oh…'

Amusement danced in Gus's eyes. 'Oh? Is that a yes or a no?'

Freya gave a flustered little laugh and gestured to her T-shirt and jeans. 'I was only thinking that I don't have a thing to wear.'

'We can find somewhere casual,' he suggested.

She thought she caught an edge of disappointment in his voice and she could well understand why he might want to spend this last evening enjoying himself. Then she remembered that she *had* brought black trousers and a couple of blouses that were almost evening wear.

'I could probably manage something better than casual.'

'Fantastic. Let's splash out on somewhere grown-up.'

* * *

Freya teamed a cream silk blouse with her black trousers and she wound her hair into a knot, which she hoped looked sophisticated, and added black hoop earrings and black toe-peepers, a black pashmina for warmth.

'Wow!' Gus grinned when he saw her. 'If that's casual, remind me to ask you to dress up some time.'

She realised that Gus had never seen her really dressed up—unless she counted the senior formal, which was so long ago he couldn't be expected to remember. She wished she was wearing high heels and stockings and something slinky and backless to make him really take notice.

Of course he looked wonderful in a dark sports jacket, white shirt and beige trousers.

'Maybe I should put a tie on,' he said, fingering the open neck of his shirt.

'No, don't. You look—' Freya could hardly say *wonderful*. 'You look fine.'

'I've wangled a late booking at a seafood restaurant near the river, and there's a taxi waiting. I didn't want to have to worry about trying to find a park.' He touched the small of Freya's back ever so lightly and she almost went into orbit as the warmth of his hand branded her skin through the thin silk fabric. 'Let's go.'

It was well after eight when they arrived, and the restaurant was very well patronised. Freya was sure every seat had been taken, but they were shown to a table for two at a window with beautiful sweeping views of the city skyline and the full beauty of the lights shining on the water.

'How on earth did you wangle such a good table at short notice?' she asked when they were alone.

Gus grinned. 'I can be quite persuasive when I put my mind to it.'

She felt a blush coming on and quickly picked up the menu. Fortunately it was large and she could almost hide behind it, studying the selection with earnest attention. The last thing she wanted now was to let her thoughts stray. There was no point in remembering how devastatingly persuasive Gus Wilder could be.

The meal was superb. Freya chose a starter of salt and pepper calamari, while Gus chose seafood chowder. Their mains were a delicate baked fish with mango and avocado salsa, and steamed crab with chilli jam.

Gus was perfect company and Freya relished this chance to sit opposite him; it gave her the perfect excuse to look into his gorgeous dark eyes whenever she wanted to. For brief moments she could almost—not quite, but *almost*—stop worrying about Nick. She could almost pretend she and Gus were dating again, and that he was in love with her.

Perhaps he knew that she'd be weepy if they talked about Nick, because he entertained her with light-hearted anecdotes about the wonderful people he'd met in Africa. He also told her about the Aboriginal elders who were working alongside him on his current building project and, because she was genuinely interested, he explained how the project worked.

'It's all about empowering the Aboriginal communities,' he said. 'In the past, they've had big, all purpose housing designs imposed on them. With this project, they're involved in every step. They decide what kind of housing they want and where it will be built. Hopefully, we avoid the culturally insensitive mistakes that have been made in the past.'

'It sounds like you're following a similar model to the one you used in Eritrea?'

'That's right. It works well. The community pitch in with the construction and there's built-in training, so the younger people are skilled in various trades. The people end up with a real sense of community ownership.'

Watching him carefully, Freya could see how very important the project was to Gus. 'I guess you'll be eager to get back to see how things are progressing.'

'I can't leave them in the lurch,' he said, answering her question obliquely.

'So you'll be heading back as soon as you're well enough?'

'That's the plan.'

Gus's eyes narrowed as if he was trying to gauge Freya's mood. She pinned on a smile and hoped it didn't look too forced.

After dinner, they walked along the path beside the river. It was such a perfectly romantic setting that they should have been holding hands but, even though they weren't, Gus walked close to Freya and the sleeve of his jacket kept brushing against the thin silk of her blouse. Each time she felt the contact she held her breath and her nerve endings went into a frenzy.

The tiniest stumble would have had her falling against the solid bulk of his chest but, as luck would have it, she walked as smoothly as a supermodel.

A light breeze blew, rippling the satin-smooth surface of the water and shattering the perfection of the reflected lights. Freya knew she should be soaking up the big-city atmosphere but, now they were away from the busy restaurant, her thoughts kept bouncing between her awareness of Gus and her worries about Nick.

'I wonder how he is,' she said.

Gus didn't have to ask what she meant. 'He's sure to be sleeping soundly,' he assured her.

'Maybe I should ring the ward to check if he's missing me?'

'But they have your mobile number. The sister promised to ring if Nick's upset.'

Freya knew Gus was right and, although she'd turned off her phone in the restaurant, she'd checked it as soon as she got outside and there were no messages, no missed calls.

She watched the stream of cars travelling over Victoria Bridge. The headlights and tail lights looked like rubies and pearls strung on necklaces.

'Nick loved the garlic necklace,' she said. 'It really helped to distract him tonight.' She came to a halt, drew a deep breath.

Gus stopped too, and he smiled at her. 'Do you remember the last time we walked beside this river?'

'Twelve years ago. You took me out to dinner, then you walked me to the station.'

And by then she'd already decided not to tell him about the baby.

Why?

Tonight, after their lovely evening together, and after the past week when Gus had slipped so easily into his role as Nick's father, it was hard to remember how she'd actually felt when she'd made such a rash, life-altering decision.

She drew a deep breath. 'Gus, before we get to the taxi rank, I want to thank you. For everything. I know you're terribly hurt that I never told you about Nick, and I'm sorry. Truly sorry. I—' Her throat was tight and she swallowed, took another breath and tried again. 'I want to thank you for being so good about it—about everything.'

To her dismay, he didn't respond and his face was in shadow now, so she couldn't even guess his reaction.

What had she expected? Sudden and total forgiveness?

Gus was helping Nick. Wasn't that enough?

Her voice was so shaky she almost sobbed. 'I also want to thank you for being such a willing donor. I wasn't sure how you'd respond after all this time.'

'It's what any father would do. I love the boy, Freya.'

'Yes, I know.'

'Besides, I have two healthy kidneys and I can manage with one. I get to give. Nick gets to live.'

'Yes.'

He made helping Nick sound like another of his well meaning and well thought out projects. Freya knew it was unreasonable to feel depressed.

Stop it, she told herself. *Be grateful for what he's doing. You can't hope for more.*

But, having him back in her life, she was so terribly aware of everything she'd given up. She hadn't only rejected Gus's lifestyle; she'd rejected

Gus—the only man she'd ever met who could fill her with happiness and longing in equal measure.

I'm greedy. His help for Nick has to be enough. I mustn't wish for more.

How many times did she have to tell herself this? When would it finally sink in?

In the back of the taxi, Gus sat beside Freya, watching the play of streetlights and shadows on her lovely face and he knew that the defences he'd been struggling to hold in place were toppling, finally and completely.

Once again, he was under Freya Jones's spell and he no longer wanted to fight it. Just the same, his timing was off. This was hardly the night to be thinking of seduction.

As if to prove it, when the taxi stopped at the hotel, Freya slipped out quickly while he paid the fare and she opened her mobile phone again.

'I've got to ring the hospital, Gus. I just have this awful feeling. I'm so frightened that something will go wrong.'

Her earnestness confirmed what he'd already known. Romance was out of the question. Hell.

How could he be thinking about anything remotely romantic when he knew Freya was desperately worried about Nick?

She'd bravely avoided talking about the boy at the restaurant, but that didn't mean she hadn't been thinking about him the whole time.

Gus knew he could say nothing to allay her fears and he watched with concern while she rang the hospital. He saw the frown creasing her smooth forehead and the dark shadow of worry in her sea-green eyes. Watched her teeth gnaw at her soft lower lip.

'Hello? It's Freya Jones. Nick's mother. I was just wondering…is everything OK?'

She was a touching picture of worried concentration as she listened to the person speaking on the other end. She looked vulnerable and yet unbearably lovely and Gus wished with everything in him that he could take away her pain and banish it for ever.

'Yes…' Freya was saying and she nodded. 'Yes… all right.' Then he saw the sudden brilliance of her smile. 'That is good news. Thank you.'

As she flipped her phone shut, she turned to

him with a beautiful happy grin. 'You were right. Nick's sound asleep and absolutely fine.'

Almost giddy with relief, she stumbled towards Gus and, without hesitation, he opened his arms to catch her.

Her silky hair brushed his cheek; her warm breasts crushed against him. He could even feel her heartbeats. Freya, after all this time…

It was beyond blissful to be hugged by Gus.

Freya felt so reassured by him and so filled with hope. She wanted to stay in his arms, absorbing his strength and protectiveness and general gorgeousness, and she never wanted to let go. Her arms seemed to be stuck to him with Velcro. Stepping away from him took a huge force of willpower, but she managed it somehow.

'Thank you,' she said, trying hard to sound normal and nonchalant. 'I needed that hug.' *Understatement of the century.*

Gus's eyes were twinkling. 'You're welcome. Any time.'

'I needed to go out tonight, too,' she told him as he opened the heavy glass doors of the hotel. 'Our dinner was perfect. I've been tense for so long, and tomorrow is going to be so…so…' She shivered. 'I would have been in such a mess if I'd had to spend tonight on my own.'

Gus placed a protective arm around her shoulders as they crossed the hotel's lobby. The concierge smiled at them—he probably thought they were lovers. Freya tried, unsuccessfully, not to mind that they weren't.

There was no one else using the lift. Gus let her enter ahead of him, which was gentlemanly, but she would have been happier if he'd kept his arm about her.

'How are you feeling?' she asked him.

To her surprise, he gave her a puzzled smile as if her question was extraordinarily difficult to answer.

'Are you nervous about tomorrow?'

'Oh.' He gave a soft self-deprecating laugh. 'Yes. Terrified.' Smiling again, he reached for her hand.

She knew he was only being playful and it was silly to get all hot and breathless about a little hand-holding.

Or was it?

Freya stole another look at Gus and his eyes

flashed a message that made her bones melt. When the lift stopped at their floor and the doors slid open, she wasn't sure that her legs would support her.

Fortunately, she made it down the hallway to her room.

'Thanks for a lovely evening, Gus.' The words felt trite, inadequate. She wanted to invite him in for coffee, or a drink, but this wasn't a date and Gus wasn't just a comfortable old friend she could relax with, so she wasn't quite sure if an invitation would be appropriate. They were in a relationship no-man's-land.

While she was dithering, Gus smiled, then reached out and gently touched the side of her face. 'You're not going to lie awake all night worrying about tomorrow, are you?'

'I…I hope not.' The touch of his fingers was electrifying.

'Maybe you shouldn't spend the night alone, Freya.'

Zap! The very thought of spending the night with him sent wave upon wave of excitement rolling through her, but he was joking, wasn't he?

Freya saw the look in his eyes—a kind of

smiling, yet serious intent. *Oh, heavens.* Maybe he wasn't joking.

Then his fingers trailed ever so gently down the side of her cheek and she knew for sure that this was something else entirely. Now she tried to remember why it wasn't a good idea to spend an entire night with Gus Wilder.

Her brain absolutely refused to cooperate.

All she could think was that this night was their only chance to be alone together, and she couldn't come up with a single reason why she should turn Gus away. He was, after all, the man who'd resided in her heart for twelve long years.

Her knees were trembling so badly she leaned against the door. 'I…I don't think I want to be alone, Gus.'

She lifted her eyes to meet his and a silent message flashed between them. Heat flared as if a thousand matches had been struck inside her. She wanted this so badly, couldn't believe it might actually be happening. When she took the key from her clutch purse, her hand was shaking and she couldn't fit it into the lock.

'Here,' Gus said gently and, taking the key, he slotted it smoothly home.

The door clicked open.

Freya stepped forward into darkness and silence, her heels sinking in luxurious thick carpeting. Gus followed and used the hotel door key to turn on the power. Immediately, the room came to life, lit by the discreet golden glow of table lamps. The air conditioner began to hum.

Freya prised her tongue from the roof of her mouth and she turned to him with a shy smile. 'Would you like coffee or a nightcap?'

'No, thanks.' He shrugged out of his jacket and tossed it onto a chair, then stepped closer and took her evening purse from her tightly clenched hands, dropped it lightly onto a glass-topped table.

Freya's heartbeats thundered. Her lips tingled with expectation as Gus's head dipped to hers. She closed her eyes and their lips touched.

Gus. At last.

The taste of him and the scent of his skin were exactly as Freya remembered. She sank into his embrace, letting his kiss flow through her like a wave breaking on the shore and washing over the sand.

It was almost too good to be true. After so many years, Gus was kissing her, holding her close to his long, hard body, holding her as if he never meant to release her.

She'd thought she might be shy or embarrassed after such a long time, but there wasn't a chance. Being with Gus felt perfectly, wonderfully *right*.

In a kind of blissful daze, they drifted towards the king-size bed and tumbled together onto the antique gold quilt. For a moment or two they just lay there, gazing into each other's eyes and smiling, as if they were eighteen again and couldn't quite believe their luck.

Gus lifted Freya's hair away from her face. 'Your eyes are still all the colours of the sea. They keep changing with your moods.'

'Your eyes don't change,' she said, looking dreamily into their chocolate depths. 'But I like them like that. Having them stay the same makes you very—'

'Predictable?'

'I was going to say grounded.' She smiled again and he smiled back and she suspected that right now, at this moment, she was as happy as she'd ever been. 'What colour are my eyes now?' she asked him.

'Sultry green.'

'Sultry?' She pouted, pretending to be disappointed.

'Stormy, then.'

'Yes, that would be right.' She wriggled closer into the arc of his body heat and a fresh tide of longing washed over her. 'I'm feeling quite stormy.'

'Me, too.'

They kissed again in the most deliciously leisurely manner, nipping, tasting, then slowly delving deeper, letting their desire rebuild in wave upon glorious wave. Then, in a burst of impatience, Freya sat up and began to undo the pearl buttons on her blouse as fast as her trembling fingers would allow.

Gus was beside her, making short work of his shirt, his shoes, his trousers. Their clothes flew about the room and the last of Freya's inhibitions went with them.

Her skin was burning as she lay down again. Gus was so beautiful and she was aching for his touch. A gasp broke from her as he knelt over her, as he lowered his head and scattered warm kisses over her jaw, over her throat and breasts.

She felt the hot sting of tears in her eyes. She

didn't want to cry, but this was Gus and her happiness was tinged with sadness too, for everything she'd lost.

'Freya.' It was only a whisper, but she caught the black note of despair in his voice. 'How did I ever let you go?'

It was too much. Her emotions spilled and she clung to him, pressing her face into his shoulder, trying to smother her tears. But Gus gently eased away from her and he kissed her damp face and her wet eyelids and then he kissed her trembling, sobbing mouth. She tasted the salt of her tears on his lips and their kiss turned wild.

Much later, Gus turned out the lamps and gathered Freya close. Holding her in the darkness, he pressed his face into the curve of her neck and breathed in the scent of her skin. Was it his imagination, or could he smell a hint of frangipani?

'Gus?' she murmured sleepily.

'Mmm?

'What are you thinking about?'

'Sparks,' he said.

'Our sparks?'

He smiled as he kissed her neck. 'Seems to

me, we don't have a problem with any lack of them.'

'Seems to me, you could be right.' Rolling onto her back, she picked up his hand and began to kiss each of his fingers. The simple intimacy wrapped around his heart and he found himself needing to confess one truth that had been nagging at him all evening.

'In case you're wondering, it wasn't like that with Monique.'

Freya stopped her kisses. 'Actually, I did wonder. I couldn't help it.'

Gus lay very still, momentarily caught between an urge to tell her everything and a desire to save himself the pain. His conscience, as always, won.

'The thing is, our marriage wasn't working too well.' He hated admitting this, but tonight—before tomorrow—he wanted Freya to know. 'In some ways, I suppose you'd say we had a marriage of convenience.'

'Really?' She was shifting in the darkness, turning and propping herself up on one elbow. 'Why?'

'Oh…it seemed like a good idea at the time.

Two young, like-minded adults living remotely in a foreign country…with healthy…needs.'

'But you weren't in love?'

After a beat, he said, 'No. I think we were fond enough, but not really in love.'

'Wouldn't it have been easier if you'd just had an affair?'

Gus smiled. Freya really was her mother's daughter. 'Is that what you'd have done?'

'I have occasionally. Very occasionally.'

'Yes, well…it sounds pretentious now, but Monique and I were trying to set a good example. Social responsibility—respectable NGOs and all that. We had an image to protect, so we thought it would be better to marry.' Even though the room was pitch-black, he closed his eyes, as if somehow that made the confession easier. 'It was a mistake.'

Gus grimaced into the darkness, not wanting to tell Freya the next bit but, now that he'd started, he needed to get the whole truth out. Not being able to see her face helped. 'That's why Monique wanted to leave Eritrea.'

'You mean she wanted to leave you?'

'Yes, she asked for a trial separation.' A sigh

escaped him. 'But my damn pride got in the way. I've never liked admitting to failure.'

'Your parents would have been upset.'

'That's putting it mildly.' His voice was rough and choked. Black clouds of despair threatened to smother him, but he forced himself to go on. 'I was totally committed to building the dam and I persuaded her to stay on for another six months, till the end of my term.'

'Oh, Gus, then the landmine happened.'

'Yes.' The word fell from his lips with a shudder.

'How awful for you.'

Gus heard the sob in Freya's voice and realised he was a fool. Why on earth had he started this conversation? Why was he trying to offload his regrets when he was supposed to be offering Freya comfort? Now he'd upset her and they were both wound up and disturbed when they were supposed to be sleeping, resting up for tomorrow.

Beside him, Freya was sitting up. 'Roll over, Gus.'

'Over?'

'Yes. You're upset and your shoulders are all tense. I'm going to give you a massage.'

'But I'm supposed to be helping you to relax.'

'You have helped, believe me.' She gave his shoulder a gentle shake. 'Now do as you're told.'

Smiling, he rolled obediently onto his stomach. 'I can't remember the last time I had a massage.'

'That's exactly why you need one now.'

Her hands began to work on his shoulders, kneading the muscles firmly and expertly in a way that was soothing rather than sexy.

Then again, Gus amended as warmth and contentment spread through him, those skilled hands were Freya's...and she *was* naked...

Morning arrived all too quickly.

Freya heard the beep of the alarm on her mobile phone and she gave a sleepy groan as she reached to turn it off. Reluctantly, she opened one eye and saw the pale light of early morning. She'd slept better than she had in months.

Then she remembered. *Oh, God*. Nick. The transplant. Gus. They had to be at the hospital early.

Chilling fear froze her.

'Morning, sleepyhead.'

Through the open doorway that led to the bathroom, she saw Gus at the basin, wearing black and white striped boxers while he shaved. One half of his jaw was clean and smooth, the other covered in white lather.

He looked amazingly relaxed and calm and, when he sent her a cheerful grin, her anxiety receded slightly. She remembered her vow to be brave and confident.

Admittedly, even with the ordeal that faced them today, she couldn't help thinking that Gus was a perfectly lovely sight to wake up to. Couldn't help admiring the very masculine way his broad shoulders and nicely defined muscles tapered down to his waist.

His skin glowed with a hint of bronze and there was a shadowing of dark hair on his chest, and every cell in her body tingled as she remembered what had happened last night. Making love with Gus had been beautiful and emotional and cathartic—every kind of wonderful.

Mmm… No wonder she'd slept so well.

But today his beautiful, strong and perfect body was going to be marred. For their son's sake.

A rush of gratitude filled her, tangling with her happiness and her fear. She swung out of bed and grabbed a towelling robe.

Hurrying over to Gus, she dodged his shaving cream and hugged him.

He chuckled softly; his arms came around her and, for just a moment, her world was perfect.

Then her fingers traced the line of ribs on his left side and she stopped at the place where the surgeon's knife would make its incision. Her stomach clenched.

She loved Gus. There was no escaping this truth. In the past she'd loved a sweet, sexy boy, but now she loved a soulful, generous and beautiful man. Whenever she was with him she felt strong and assured. Right at this moment, she was ready to fight dragons, to trek through dark jungles or endure four hours alone while today's surgery took place.

Forcing her fear aside, Freya smiled up at him bravely and she kissed him, shaving cream and all.

CHAPTER NINE

FREYA'S assurance faltered at the hospital's admissions desk. Gus expected her to abandon him here, but how could she?

'I don't need your help to fill in a form,' he told her gently. 'You hurry on to see Nick. He needs you now.'

'But I'll try to get back to you before you go to Theatre.'

'Stay with Nick, Freya. I'll be fine.'

She'd never felt so torn. She was desperate to see Nick, but it was so hard to leave Gus. Above his lopsided smile, his dark eyes seemed to smoulder and glow, as if his emotions were as riotous as hers.

'If I don't make it back before you go down to the theatre...' Freya hesitated, fighting tears while her heart played leapfrog with her stomach. She wanted to tell Gus she loved him but the admissions nurse was watching them and, besides, Gus might not want to hear her confession. Mightn't he be shocked that she'd jumped to conclusions about their relationship after just one night together?

'All the best,' she offered instead. 'Good luck, Gus. Break a leg.'

With a soft sound that might have been a groan, he pulled her into his arms and hugged her.

'Thanks,' she whispered into his shirt. 'Another hug just might get me through this.'

'Me, too.'

Releasing her, he gave her a wink and dropped a warm, comforting kiss on her cheek. 'Off you go. Give my love to Nick. And don't forget to grab a coffee. You're not expected to fast just because we have to.'

No way could Freya drink coffee—her stomach was churning. As she hurried away, the happiness and confidence that had buoyed her since she'd woken crumbled hopelessly and her fear returned.

Doubts rushed back. Today was going to be such a huge emotional strain. How could she stay strong for hours and hours? What if anything went wrong? Could she bear it?

She wanted to be brave—she *had* to be brave—but what could be scarier than having the two people she loved most in the entire world undergoing major surgery?

Outside Nick's room, she stopped and took a deep breath. Nick was so quick to pick up on her mood. Her reaction became his reaction, so she couldn't let him see any sign of her fear. Squeezing her face muscles, she fixed her smile into place.

To her relief, the smile held as she breezed through the doorway.

'Hey, Mum.' Nick was beaming. 'Look who's here.'

Freya's smile slipped when she saw the dignified silver-haired couple standing by her son's bed. The man was in a grey suit, the woman a picture of elegant conservatism in navy linen and pearls. It had been years—but she recognised them instantly.

Gus's parents.

Freya's hand leapt to press against her rioting heartbeats. Of course, she'd known that at some stage she would have to face up to Bill and

Deirdre Wilder, but she hadn't expected to see them this morning.

'My grandmother and my grandfather have come to see me,' Nick announced proudly. 'They're Gus's parents and they've flown all the way from Western Australia.'

Freya managed a shaky smile and extended her hand. 'Mr and Mrs Wilder, how lovely to see you again.'

Gus's parents nodded. His mother's eyes, which were the same dark brown as Gus's, regarded Freya sternly.

At least they returned her handshakes.

Gus's father nodded solemnly. 'How do you do, Freya?'

'Hello, Freya.' His mother spoke cautiously and without smiling.

'It's wonderful that you could get here so quickly.' Freya spoke in her warmest tones. 'You must have flown all night.'

Deirdre Wilder's mouth tilted awkwardly as she smoothed a non-existent crease in her navy linen jacket. 'Actually, we arrived last night. We tried to ring Angus at his hotel, but we couldn't seem to raise him.'

Freya couldn't miss the mild accusation in her tone.

'Is Gus all right?' This question was fired by Gus's father.

'Oh, yes.' Freya gulped. 'He's being admitted right now, as we speak.'

Freya hoped she didn't look guilty. No doubt the Wilders already viewed her as the scarlet woman who'd seduced their son and stolen their grandchild. She knew it was silly, but she couldn't shake off the feeling that they'd also guessed that their son had spent last night in her bed.

In the awkward pause that followed, Freya said, 'You have no idea how grateful I am—how grateful both Nick and I are. If it wasn't for Gus…' She had to stop as tears threatened. She was very aware that this situation was as hugely emotional for Gus's parents as it was for her.

Taking a deep breath, she slipped an arm around Nick's shoulders. 'Now Nick gets to meet his grandparents.'

As much to reassure herself as anyone, she bent to kiss Nick's cheek and she couldn't resist stroking his hair. 'So how are you feeling, champ?'

'Hungry. The nurses won't let me have any breakfast.'

Freya smiled. 'Gus can't eat anything either.'

Deirdre Wilder said in a choked voice, 'Nick looks so much like Angus.'

'Poppy always says my eyes are like Mum's.' Nick was lapping up being the focus of everyone's attention, and Freya found that she was grateful for any distraction from the impending operation.

'Well, yes…your eyes are quite light.' Deirdre Wilder smiled at Nick with surprising gentleness, although a chill crept into her features as she turned to Freya. 'Is your mother here, Freya?'

Deirdre managed to look down her nose as she said this, as if she'd clearly expected Poppy Jones to renege on her grandmotherly duties.

'Poppy's on her way,' Freya said. 'She's coming down on the train this morning.' She gave Nick another reassuring smile. 'Poppy will be waiting to see you when you wake up.'

Truth be told, Freya had been surprised when Poppy hadn't insisted on coming to Brisbane at the same time that she and Gus had driven down with Nick. But her mother had been adamant that Nick, Freya and Gus needed time alone together.

'To bond,' Poppy had said with mysterious significance. 'I'll mind Urchin till then. Then Nick's friend Jamie will have him, and I'll jump on the train first thing on the day of the operation. I'll be ready for Nick when he needs me most.'

Freya wondered how much 'bonding' her mother had anticipated. She suspected that Poppy was feeling a tad guilty about her insistence all those years ago that her daughter didn't need a man in her life, that they could raise Nick just fine on their own.

Whatever her mother's reasons had been, Freya was beyond grateful for that time with Gus. Heavens, how could she have dreamed they would become so close, so quickly? But it would be impossible to explain any of this to Deirdre Wilder.

Sudden footsteps outside announced the arrival of a nurse.

'Good morning, Nick.' She breezed into the room with a bright nursey smile. 'I've come to wash you with special soap and to dress you in this gown.' Grinning, she held up a green cotton hospital gown. 'What do you think of the latest fashion?'

Nick eyed it dubiously. 'Will my dad have to wear one of those, too?'

'He's probably getting into his right about now,' the nurse said. 'And without any argument.'

Deirdre Wilder stiffened and turned to her husband. 'We'd better hurry if we want to see Angus.'

There was a flurry of kisses and calls from the door of 'good luck, darling', and then Gus's parents were gone.

As the nurse began to unbutton Nick's pyjamas, he sent Freya a satisfied grin. 'Now I've got a father and four grandparents. How cool is that? I'm like Jamie Galloway now.'

Seeing the shining excitement in her son's eyes, Freya felt her throat tighten painfully. She wanted to tell Nick that he mustn't expect that his family would suddenly be like Jamie Galloway's.

Jamie, Nick's best friend, had both sets of his grandparents living right in the Sugar Bay hinterland. Both families had cane farms and they hosted huge get-togethers at Christmas and on birthdays. Their homesteads regularly overflowed with aunts and uncles and cousins, and Nick viewed these family gatherings as his version of heaven.

It was impossible to imagine that the Joneses and the Wilders would ever get together for something like that. But, as the nurse began to wash Nick, the boy grinned at Freya.

'Actually, I'm even luckier than Jamie. His dad hasn't given him a kidney.'

Oh, help. Freya almost sobbed aloud. Instead, she focused on giving him another brave smile.

Almost as soon as Nick was bathed and dressed, a friendly young anaesthetist arrived to insert an IV line into his arm.

'This is where the medicine goes while you're having the operation,' the doctor told him.

Nick paled as he eyed the tubes and syringe. 'Is my dad having these in him, too?'

'I've just finished fitting his.'

That was enough to satisfy Nick and he submitted without a grimace. Freya wished she could rush back to Gus to tell him how wonderfully reassured Nick was, just knowing that his dad was sharing his ordeal.

But she wouldn't leave Nick now. Besides, the

thought of Gus's parents watching her interaction with their son made her distinctly nervous.

To Gus's shame, his spirits took a dive when the footsteps in the corridor materialised into his parents. He hadn't expected to see Freya again, but a guy could always hope. How had his folks got here so soon?

'Angus,' his mother sobbed, rushing to hug him. 'You poor darling.'

'Whoops. Watch the IV tube, Mum.'

Gus submitted to her hugs and to his father's handshakes and backslaps.

'Are you OK, son?'

'Yes, I'm fine, thanks. I've had so many health checks lately.' He managed to crack a grin. 'Seems I'm close to perfect.'

His mother chatted nervously while she stroked his hair as if he were ten years old—although Gus couldn't actually remember her being so demonstrative when he was a kid and had longed for signs of affection.

'We had to see you before you went down to Theatre,' she said. 'But we've met Nick, and he's a lovely boy, isn't he? He's so much like you.'

'How's he doing?' Gus asked, hoping his mother hadn't upset the boy. 'Is he OK?'

'Oh, yes. He's being very brave. And we saw Freya, of course. She looks—'

'Is she OK, too?' Gus interjected. Despite his concern for Nick, it was Freya who filled his head. Poor girl, she must be so stressed right now.

His mother's mouth pursed, sour lemon tight. 'Freya looks well.' She managed to make Freya's glowing health sound like a character fault.

Gus's father cleared his throat. 'You're doing the right thing, son. Your mother and I want you to know we're proud of you.'

'Thanks, Dad.' Gus's gratitude was genuine. 'Thanks for coming.'

He'd half-expected to be hammered by questions—about why Freya hadn't told him about their grandson, and would they have ever known about Nick if he hadn't needed a transplant?

He could just hear his mother's questions. *What's happening about access? Freya can't keep you out of Nick's life any more, Gus.*

No doubt the questions would come later.

Something to look forward to, Gus thought, mentally wincing.

'Now, don't worry about a thing,' Deirdre said. 'We'll be here to look after you once you're through with this.'

'There's no need. I'll be—'

'Of course there's every need, darling. We've come all this way, just to care for you. You've been looking after other people for far too long. It's time you had some pampering.'

That might be so, but the only pampering that interested Gus was the kind that involved Freya. He wasn't going to argue about it now though, and he was rather relieved when two male nurses arrived.

'Time to take you down to Theatre,' they announced cheerily.

At last. Gus was keen to get on with it. In vain, he tried to reassure his mother, who'd begun to cry. 'Don't worry. I'll be fine.'

Tears streamed down her face as she waved him goodbye.

'Keep an eye on Freya,' he called.

His mother cried harder than ever.

It was the longest day of Freya's life.

While Gus's surgery commenced, she waited

with Nick in his room. He played with his Game Boy and she tried to read a magazine, but she couldn't concentrate on photos of celebrities pushing babies in prams or holidaying in the South of France. And, although Nick madly pressed the buttons on his tiny screen, his face expressed none of his usual enjoyment in high-speed battles with aliens.

One good thing—the doctors in the operating theatre sent word back that Gus's procedure was going according to plan, and that was a wonderful relief. Then it was Nick's turn to go down to Theatre.

Freya's stomach flip-flopped. This was the moment she'd dreaded but, for Nick's sake, she had to hold up a brave front. She thought of Gus, already down at Theatre, giving up his kidney, and she clung to the doctors' assurance that everything was going well. Nick was simply going down there to receive Gus's gift. That was all.

When this was over, Nick would be healthy again and, with luck, he would go on living healthily for a very, very long time.

But, as he was lifted onto a trolley, he looked impossibly young and small and vulnerable.

She remembered the day he was born and how she'd fallen instantly in love with his tiny pink perfection.

Tears prickled her eyelids. She ignored them. 'Off you go, then,' she said, lightly kissing him goodbye as if he was heading off to school or to a football game. 'Poppy will be here when you wake up.'

Nick tried to smile but his face was pale and worried as he disappeared around a corner.

Freya was left alone.

Too anxious to sit still, she paced the corridors. She passed a water fountain and realised she hadn't had anything to drink all morning. Sipping iced water from a paper cup, she told herself again that everything would be fine. Nick and Gus were in good hands. Even so, her insides were hollow with dread.

She should probably eat something, or at least get a coffee from a vending machine, but the very thought of ingesting anything stronger than water made her ill. She tried to ring Poppy, who would be midway through her train journey to Brisbane by now. The sound of her mother's warm, smoky voice would be such a comfort, but she couldn't get through. Poppy hated modern technology and hardly ever turned on her mobile phone.

Leaving a message, Freya continued her pacing. She was desperate to stay positive so she pictured Nick in the future, living with Gus's kidney, happy and well. *No rejections, please, please...*

She imagined Nick graduating from university, getting a plum job and getting married, becoming a father. She so wanted her boy's life to be perfect in every way. She would have to be careful not to interfere. She would let Nick make his own decisions, his own choices. She only hoped he'd make wiser choices than she had.

When it came to thinking about Gus, however, Freya couldn't picture his future, or perhaps she was afraid to. Her mind seemed to freeze whenever she tried. Could she dare to hope or was that totally foolish?

She wished she'd talked to Gus about the future last night when she'd had the chance. But he'd offered her nothing more than one night, and that night had been so fabulous, she hadn't wanted to spoil the magic.

Of course, she couldn't help reliving all the lovely memories. Gus's special mix of tenderness and passion couldn't be faked, surely? Her heart did a tumble turn every time she thought about it, especially when she thought about his surprising confession about his marriage. Poor man. Guilt, even when it wasn't really warranted, was a heavy burden to carry.

She tried to hold the memories close, like a protective fire blanket around her vulnerable heart, but already the night was beginning to feel like a dream. Had it been too good to be true?

All she actually knew about Gus's plans was that he was going back to the Northern Territory as soon as he was well enough, and his project would take months to complete. There was nothing in that scenario that encouraged rosy dreams.

Reluctantly, she turned her thoughts to Deirdre and Bill Wilder, who were no doubt sitting quietly and sensibly in the waiting room, as they'd been told to, as any news from the theatre would be relayed there.

So what am I doing, trying to avoid them and blundering around in corridors?

Dismayed by her foolishness, Freya hurried back down the maze of corridors. Twice she got lost, but eventually she arrived at the waiting room, shaking and rather breathless.

There was no sign of Gus's parents.

CHAPTER TEN

THE family group sitting in the corner of the waiting room turned in unison when Freya came in.

'I'm sorry to trouble you,' she said. 'I…I don't suppose you saw an older couple waiting in here?'

'Their son was having surgery, but he's out now,' a woman told her. 'They've gone back with him to his room.'

'Oh.' Adrenaline made Freya's heart pound. 'Thank you.'

She felt sick as she hurried back down the highly waxed corridors, pausing at the nurse's desk to ask where Gus's room was, then speeding on as quickly as her shaky legs allowed.

When she reached Gus's room, she caught a glimpse of him lying in the bed, apparently asleep and with a distressing number of tubes attached to him. He was flanked by his mother and his father, and Deirdre Wilder rose quickly and hurried to the door on tiptoe, a finger raised to her lips, her eyes fierce, demanding silence.

'Angus shouldn't be disturbed,' she hissed.

'Is he OK?'

Frowning elaborately, Deirdre stepped out into the corridor. 'He came through the operation splendidly, but he's sleeping off the anaesthetic. The nurses warned us he'll need strong painkillers and they might make him sleepy.'

'Poor Gus.'

'Indeed,' Deirdre said tightly.

Peering over Deirdre's shoulder, Freya saw Gus's eyes flicker open. 'Can I go in, just for a moment?'

'Under the circumstances, I think Angus's father and I are the best people to help him now.'

'I'd just like to—'

'He may be well enough to receive visitors later.' Gus's mother's eyes were hard and decidedly unfriendly. 'For short periods.'

Her meaning was clear. *We're Gus's family and you, Freya Jones, are a rank outsider and more trouble than you're worth.*

'Please give him my best,' Freya said, but she

very much doubted that her request would be granted.

Unsure how much longer she could hold it together, Freya went back to the waiting room. She still had ages to wait and she feared she might cave in before the time was up.

But Poppy was there.

And what a sudden, uncomplicated joy it was to see her mother, swathed in her customary colourful layers. How lovely to be welcomed into her familiar embrace.

At last the waiting became almost bearable. Poppy had brought a basket with a Thermos of tea, still surprisingly hot, and a tin of shortbread made by the mother of one of Nick's school friends. She talked about Sugar Bay—about the glorious weather they'd had this past few days, how Urchin had been happy to stay at Jamie Galloway's while she was away, and how she'd been inundated with calls from well-wishers.

The snippets of gossipy news from home were a welcome diversion and Poppy didn't ask prying questions about the past few days, for which Freya was especially grateful.

Somehow they got through the remaining hours

and, eventually, Dr Lee appeared at the doorway. Freya's heart jolted as she leapt to her feet.

'Things couldn't be better,' he said. 'The kidney's in place and everything's working. Nick's already making urine on the table.' He grinned at them. 'He's peeing like a racehorse.'

'How wonderful!' Freya hugged him and thanked him, and she hugged her mother and thanked her. 'What about Gus?' she asked. 'Does he know the good news?'

Dr Lee shook his head. 'Not yet.'

'Then you must excuse me.' She was already at the door. 'I'll have to go and tell him.'

Freya began to run.

The pain was bad.

Gus had been prepared for it but the severity was still a shock. He woke, fighting it, and opened his eyes to find his mother sitting beside his bed. 'How's Nick?' was the first thing he wanted to know.

'We haven't heard yet, darling.'

Gus closed his eyes, needing all his strength just to deal with the pain. He felt drugged and he drifted in and out of sleep. At one time when he woke he was aware of whispers and he thought he heard Freya's voice. His eyes snapped open.

His mother was at the door, but now she came silently back to the side of his bed.

'Was that Freya?'

'Yes, dear. She came to tell us that everything went very well with Nick. He's out of the theatre and on his way to the children's intensive care, but he's fine.'

'Ohhhh… that's great.' Gus managed to crack a grin. 'That's fabulous. I'm so glad.' Then he remembered. 'Why didn't she come in to see me?'

'You need to rest, darling.'

'You mean you sent her away?' He tried to sit up and gasped as fiery pain ripped through his left side.

'You're not ready for visitors,' his mother said.

Gus wanted to disagree, but a wave of exhaustion hit him and he hadn't the strength to argue.

'That Wilder woman's always been a dragon,' Poppy told Freya. 'And she hasn't mellowed with age.'

'I was thinking she was more like a Rottweiler.'

Mother and daughter shared rueful smiles over the dinner table. There was nothing more they could do at the hospital overnight while Nick and Gus rested in expert care, so they'd come away for an evening meal.

'Pasta is wonderful comfort food,' Poppy had declared as they passed tempting smells from an Italian restaurant. Thus, here they were at a corner table with a crisp white cloth and gleaming silver, each with a glass of Sauvignon Blanc and deep bowls of divine melt-in-the-mouth gnocchi Gorgonzola.

It was the first proper meal Freya had eaten all day and she felt herself finally beginning to unwind. Perhaps that was why she was so willing to express her disappointment about Gus's mother.

'She won't let me near Gus. She blocked me like a footballer.'

Poppy dismissed this with a hand-waving gesture that made her silver bracelets tinkle. 'She won't be able to stop him from getting near you once he has his strength back.'

'I wouldn't be too sure about that.'

'Oh, Freya, stop being so negative.'

Freya sighed. She was feeling strangely 'out of it' and exhausted now that most of the tension had left her. Of course, a degree of tension would continue for some time while they waited to see if Nick's body would accept the new kidney, but so far the indications were excellent.

Why couldn't she feel happier? She'd expected to be elated tonight. She should be elated. She'd been waiting for this day for such a long time and now the weeks of longing and dread were behind her. In a couple of weeks, Nick and Gus could resume their normal lives.

That was the problem, wasn't it? Gus's normal life was far off in the Northern Territory, and she was going to miss him horribly. And the gnawing dissatisfaction that she felt at the end of this day of triumph was caused solely by the fact that she hadn't been able to see him.

She hadn't been able to look into his eyes the way she had with Nick, to see for herself that he really was OK. Hadn't been able to reassure herself that his feelings for her were still as strong as they'd been this morning.

Shame on you, Freya. The poor man's in pain and you're being disgustingly selfish.

'Stop worrying, Freya.' Poppy was frowning at her and her voice expressed an edge of impatience.

'Sorry. I think I must be down because I'm so tired.' Freya reached over and squeezed her mum's hand. 'You know what you've always said. Everything always seems better after a good night's sleep. I'll be right as rain tomorrow.'

Gus couldn't believe his mother was back on guard duty early next morning. Not that she saw her ministrations in that light, of course. She arrived with flowers and fruit and three paperback novels, and set up camp in the corner of Gus's room as if she planned to read her women's magazine from cover to cover and had no intention of shifting.

Gus loved his mother, of course he did, but she had an unfortunate habit of trying to smother. This trait had been behind his escape to Africa, while his sister had taken off to Perth on the other side of the continent, only to have their parents follow.

Now he suppressed a groan of irritation. He wasn't an invalid. The IV tubes had been removed and he'd been up and had a shower and he was eager to get on with his recovery.

'Mum, you're not expected to stay here all day,' he said in his most diplomatic tones.

'Oh, darling, I don't mind. It's such a long time since I've been able to do anything for you. I want to be on hand in case you need anything.' She gave his hand a possessive pat. 'Anything at all.'

'Well, to be honest, what I need most is to see Nick.'

Her eyes widened. 'Well, of course, that would be lovely. I believe he's out of Intensive Care and back in his room.'

'Great.' Gus threw off the bed sheet.

'But you can't be thinking of walking to him, Angus. You're not strong enough.'

'Of course I am.'

Alarmed, his mother dropped the magazine. 'No! Wait! I'll see if I can find a wheelchair.'

'I don't need a wheelchair.'

'But you do.' Her voice was becoming querulous. 'Don't be foolish about this. I'll go and make enquiries.'

Gus wasn't prepared to wait. He wanted to see Nick and, for crying out loud, he wanted to get there under his own steam, not to be pushed along by his mother. As soon as she'd left, he eased himself cautiously out of bed. The soreness under his left ribs was still pretty grim, but he would just have to put up with it.

He could walk quite well if he held himself very straight.

It was Poppy who greeted Gus in Nick's room. 'Gus, how wonderful to see you up and about. Nick, look who's here.' Her face broke into a beaming smile and she hurried to the door and took his elbow.

'Easy does it, hero,' she murmured in an undertone as she guided him to a chair, which he sank into gratefully. 'I'll leave you two to have a nice chat,' she said, then discreetly retreated outside.

Gus took in the boy's bright eyes and healthy colour. 'Nick, you look fantastic.'

'I feel great. Dr Lee said my new kidney is in better shape than his.'

'How about that?'

'Thanks, Dad,' Nick said softly.

To Gus's dismay, he felt the sting of tears. *Damn it*, he loved this kid so much and he'd been so scared this transplant wouldn't work. He forced a shaky smile. 'Knowing you're going to be well is the best news I've ever had.'

The boy's eyes shone. 'Sister says I can get up later today.'

'Amazing.'

Without warning, Nick's smile vanished. 'But there's one bad thing.'

'What's that?' Gus asked, heart sinking.

'I can't play tackle football any more.'

The relief that the problem was so small made Gus want to smile. But he hadn't forgotten how he'd felt at Nick's age, when rugby league had dominated his life and he'd dreamed of playing for the Australian Kangaroos. 'That's a low blow.' He gave Nick's shoulder a gentle punch. 'But you know what it means, don't you?'

Nick pouted. 'What?'

'You'll have more time for surfing, and for being a lifesaver, and for climbing mountains and sailing oceans, chasing girls…'

At the mention of girls, the boy giggled.

'Speaking of girls,' Gus said, hoping his voice sounded casual, 'where's your mum?' He *had* to ask. In spite of everything else, he couldn't stop thinking about Freya and the question burned in him.

'She had to go and make phone calls. Something to do with the gallery. She should be back soon.' The boy was watching Gus with a carefully knowing gaze.

'What's that look for?' Gus asked.

'I was thinking maybe you do still like Mum.'

'Well, of course I like her.' The back of Gus's neck grew hot.

'But does that mean—?' Nick flushed and looked awkwardly down at his hands as he twisted a corner of the bed sheet between his fingers. 'I don't suppose…I mean…are you thinking about marrying her?'

Slam! It was like running into an invisible brick wall. The last thing Gus had expected was that his son, barely out of Intensive Care, would morph into a matchmaker.

Somehow, he manufactured a chuckle to cover

his consternation. 'You're jumping the gun, aren't you, mate?'

'What do you mean?'

'You're rushing things.' Gus scratched his jaw as he tried to figure how to handle this question. Of course, it would be helpful if he knew the answer.

Despite the pain and his parents' visits and the intrusions of the hospital staff, he hadn't stopped thinking about Freya. The night he'd spent with her had been incredible, even better than when they were young. One night with Freya could never be enough.

But they needed time to discover where this fabulous chemistry might take them.

They didn't have time. Not for romance.

And he didn't want to give Nick false hope or confuse him. The kid needed a chance to heal, to stabilize at home with his mother and grand-mother…to ease back into school life…and into a new sport…

Gus suppressed a grimace. Nick was watching his every reaction with the intensity of Sigmund Freud combined with Sherlock Holmes.

'Since your mother and I met up again in

Darwin, our focus has been on you,' Gus said. 'All my time's been taken up with getting you better. I haven't had much chance to think about other things, like romance…or…or marriage.'

'But you have time now, don't you?'

'Not really, Nick. As soon as I can, I have to get back to my work in the Northern Territory. A whole community is depending on me.'

The boy's face fell and Gus hastened to mollify him. 'But I'll be staying in touch with you…and… with your mum.'

Nick nodded very slowly, as if he needed to think this through. 'Are you still angry with Mum for not telling you about me?'

Gus let out his breath on a whoosh. 'No,' he said after a bit. 'Not any more. I think I stopped being upset about that as soon as I got to know you.'

The boy smiled shyly.

'But you shouldn't be bothering your head about these things.' Gus ruffled Nick's hair.

'I'm not really worried.'

'Good.'

'Thing is, I reckon I've worked out what probably happened between you and Mum, and why she never told you about me.'

'No kidding?' Was there no end to the surprises with this kid? Gus couldn't help asking. 'So? Maybe you'd better fill me in?'

'Well…something happened at school.' Nick dropped his gaze. 'Everyone knew why I had to go to hospital and on the last day…this girl in my class…' He shot Gus a quick glance. 'She's usually quiet and sort of sensible.'

'They're often the best sort,' Gus said, biting back an urge to smile.

'Anyway, when I was leaving,' Nick went on, 'she ran after me and called out, to wish me good luck.'

'She sounds nice.'

'Yeah, I know.' The boy's mouth developed an embarrassed lopsided twist. 'The thing is, I didn't do anything. I went all weird. I pretended I didn't hear her. I wanted to say something back, but I just kept walking with my head down, like a… like a…'

'Numbskull?'

'Yeah.'

'And now you wish you'd handled it better?'

The boy nodded.

Gus swallowed to ease the log jam in his throat. 'Don't worry. You'll be able to say something nice to her when you get back.'

'If I'm brave enough.'

'You're a brave kid. Never doubt that.' Gus smiled. 'So you think that I probably stuffed up when I was young, and never said the right thing to your mum?'

'Well…maybe.'

Out of the mouths of babes. Gus sighed, remembering the day he'd put Freya on the train, remembering his dismay when he realised, as it drew out of the station, that she was crying.

If only he'd found out why…

His life might have been so different.

He might not have graduated. He certainly wouldn't have gone to Africa…or been involved in fascinating projects in distant parts.

Freya's life would have been so very different too. She'd spent so many years battling on her own.

Hell… The truth of this was like a sounding bell deep inside Gus. He saw Freya's decision to keep the pregnancy a secret in a whole new light.

Truth was…when he'd made her pregnant, he'd stolen the future she'd planned. But, by remaining silent, she'd handed him his future as a gift.

He sent Nick a rueful smile. 'You could be right,' he said softly. 'Maybe being a numbskull runs in the family?'

Nick grinned at him, but then his attention was caught by someone at the door. 'Oh, hi, Mum.'

Gus whirled around, wincing as pain scorched through his left side. He could tell by the look on Freya's face that she'd heard at least some of their conversation.

Her smile was awkward as she came into the room. 'It's just wonderful to see you two on the mend so soon.'

Pink tinged her cheeks as she perched on the edge of Nick's bed. She was wearing an outfit Gus particularly liked—jeans and a soft grey cardigan that should have looked schoolmarmish, but on Freya looked incredibly attractive. Make that sexy.

'I came across Poppy and your mum down the

hall,' she told him. 'They seemed to be involved in a cold war over a wheelchair.'

Gus groaned. 'That's mothers for you. Mine's determined to strap me into that thing and wheel me around like a baby.' He pulled a face that made Nick laugh, then sent the boy a surreptitious wink. 'I'm setting you a bad example here, so don't take any notice.'

To Freya, he said, 'Do you think you could escort me back to my room? I'd be safe with you. I can't imagine that my mother would arm wrestle with you just to get me into that blasted chair.'

Freya gulped as if she'd swallowed a beetle, but eventually she recovered enough to say, 'Of course. I'm happy to help.'

Her skin tightened all over and her cheeks burned as she helped Gus out of the chair.

He was wearing a dressing gown over striped pyjamas, and he looked a little pale and he certainly moved cautiously, but none of these things could diminish his masculinity, or the effect of his proximity on her heartbeats.

After flashing a farewell grin at Nick, they set off with Gus folding Freya's arm through his and holding it close against his good side. She

savoured the warmth of him and the now familiar smell of his aftershave but, coming on top of
overhearing his conversation with Nick, it was
all rather overwhelming.

This morning she'd woken to a huge sense of
anticlimax. Now she was back to feeling tense,
hot and bothered.

In the corridor, they found Poppy alone.

'You're off the hook, Gus. A nurse finally convinced your mother that it's desirable for fit pa-
tients like you to be up and walking as soon as
possible after surgery, so she's taken the wheelchair back.'

'Bless the nurse,' Gus said.

Poppy laughed. 'Your mum took some convincing.'

She sent Freya a bright, pleased smile, which
Freya did her best to ignore. Her mother was
almost as bad as Nick when it came to wanting
to see her and Gus reunited. No way did she want
Poppy to read too much into this simple act of
walking Gus back to his room.

Freya half-expected Gus to release her now the
wheelchair threat was gone, but he tucked her

arm more tightly beneath his and when he smiled at her his eyes smouldered sexily.

Deep down, she was totally, over-the-top thrilled by this simple contact, but she was also scared and on edge. Now that the transplant was behind them, she had no idea where their relationship stood. She wasn't even sure they had a relation-ship and she didn't want to start hoping, only to be disappointed.

But poor Gus could hardly be expected to think about romance after everything he'd been through. He looked pale and exhausted by the time they reached his room.

'You need to rest now,' Freya said after she'd helped him back onto the bed and given him a drink from the water jug.

'I'm fine.' He reached for her hand. 'Please, don't rush away. I've hardly seen you and we need to talk.' He patted a space on the bed beside him. 'Sit here.'

Time alone with Gus was like discovering gold, so of course Freya sat, even though she was sure he really needed to rest. Her heartbeats went hay-wire as she wondered what he wanted to talk about. The other night, after they'd made love, they'd talked about his marriage but they hadn't talked about their own relationship, past, present or future.

Of course, they talked about Nick—quietly relieved that the worst was behind them.

Gus's fingers touched the back of her hand. 'You know I'm going to miss you.'

Freya wasn't sure if she was pleased that he would miss her, or sorry that he was already thinking ahead to when he would leave for the Northern Territory.

'You won't be heading off for a while yet, will you?'

'I'm hoping to get away next week.'

'So soon?'

'The doctors aren't thrilled about it, and if my parents had their way I'd spend another week at the Gold Coast with them. But I'm confident I'll be fine, and I need to get back.'

Freya nodded, tried to smile.

'The people up there are trusting me,' he said. 'Politicians have let them down in the past, but I'm determined to keep my word. We can't afford any more delays, and we have to get the work completed before the start of the wet season.'

It made perfect sense, of course. From the start, Freya had known she was dragging Gus away from important work, and he'd already given her so-o-o-o much. She had no right to be disappointed.

'Nick and I will have to stay here in Brisbane for a few more weeks,' she said. 'Even after Nick gets out of hospital, he has to have daily blood tests to check for rejection.'

'He wouldn't dare to reject my kidney.'

'Oh, God, I hope not.'

Gently, Gus smiled and he touched her cheek. 'Don't worry, Floss.'

Floss. Her old nickname. Freya loved that he remembered. His hand cupped her face and she felt a warm rush of happiness. All it took was Gus's smile and his touch and her heart was flying. She closed her eyes and pressed her cheek into his palm.

'To be honest, I've had enough of worrying,' she said. 'From now on I'm going to have perfect faith that your wonderful gift will keep Nick well for ever.'

'Absolutely.' His thumb roamed lazily over her skin. 'I've promised Nick I'll stay in touch.'

'That will mean a lot to him.'

'And, with luck, this job should be finished by Christmas.'

Six weeks away. Even though Freya knew the time would fly, it still felt such a long time to wait. And there was no guarantee that Gus would come rushing straight to the Bay as soon as he was free. 'I guess your family will expect you to spend Christmas with them.' She tried not to sound downhearted.

'They might.' Gus's fingers traced the shape of her ear lobe now. 'But I might have to disappoint them. A very important member of my family lives in Sugar Bay.'

He was talking about Nick, of course.

'Perhaps you shouldn't get Nick's hopes up about Christmas,' Freya said quietly. 'Just in case you can't make it.'

'You're worried I'll disappoint him, the way your father did.'

'We certainly wouldn't want another Christmas disaster.'

'I promise I won't let the boy down, Freya.' Gus slipped his hand behind her neck and his fingers rubbed her nape. 'And I won't let you down.'

What did that mean, exactly?

Before Freya could work out the best way to ask Gus, he drew her face closer to his. She saw the mix of passion and tenderness in his eyes and her heart began to dance.

Gus gave her a rueful smile. 'Come closer,' he murmured. 'I want to kiss you and I can't unless you lean in.'

'Are your ribs hurting?'

'A bit.'

'Maybe you shouldn't excite yourself,' she said, even though she leaned closer and her blood began to fizz.

'Maybe a little excitement is just what the doctor ordered.'

Their noses were almost touching. Their lips brushed. Freya's body shot sparks. 'And why should I let you kiss me?' she whispered, partly to tease him and partly because she really needed to know.

'Good heavens!' a woman's voice shrilled from behind them. 'Gus will open up his stitches. What on earth do you think you're doing?'

Freya flinched and she heard Gus's groan. His

mother stormed into the room like a battleship with cannons blazing.

Freya wanted to echo Gus's groan. Now she'd confirmed Deirdre Wilder's worst fear that she was a brazen hussy, intent on seducing Gus over to the Dark Side.

'I can't believe—' Deirdre began.

'Mum, please, you've said quite enough. We're not children.'

Gus's air of cool command clearly surprised his mother. Her self-righteous lips flapped for a beat or two, then snapped unhappily closed.

Taking her cue from Gus, Freya threw off the feeling that she'd been caught in flagrante delicto, and she rose from the bed with perfect dignity. She caught Gus's eye, read his flash of apology.

'As I was saying,' she told Gus, 'you really do need to rest.'

'Don't worry, I plan to.'

Freya smiled. 'I'll leave you to it, then.' She smiled at his mother and said, ever so politely, 'Good morning, Mrs Wilder.'

When there was no response, she slipped quietly from the room.

Once outside, she allowed herself to recall every

detail of her precious moments with Gus, right to the breathtaking second before he almost kissed her.

Her face broke into a smile and she gave a little skip, happier than she'd been in months.

Gus eyed his mother squarely. 'I'm sorry, but you can't go on like this, Mum. Do you realise how over the top you were then?'

'I was only worrying about you. Freya's worried about Nick. I'm worried about you.'

He nodded. 'I appreciate that, but there was more to it than that. You've still got a problem with Freya and Poppy, haven't you?'

'A problem with their lifestyle.' Deirdre's shoulders lifted in a half-hearted shrug. 'It's always been so different. So casual.'

'But you have to admit Nick's a wonderful boy,' Gus said. 'I'm proud to be his father.'

'Oh, yes, dear. You're quite right. He's adorable.'

'Well behaved,' Gus added. 'Thoughtful and courageous.'

'Of course.'

'And you have to remember that he didn't get to

be like that on his own, and yet we had nothing to do with his upbringing.'

Deirdre opened her mouth as if she wanted to say something, then shut it as she changed her mind.

'If Nick's turned out well, it's thanks to Freya and Poppy,' Gus said. 'I think Freya's done a remarkable job, and I'd really like you to ease off on her.'

Looking distinctly abashed, Deirdre nodded her silent agreement.

Satisfied, Gus closed his eyes as a wave of exhaustion washed over him. He began to drift towards sleep, thinking about Freya and Nick and Poppy, about what an effective unit they were. He wondered how exactly he could fit into that picture.

But the big question was—should he revisit that territory? What if he tried to get back with Freya and it didn't work? Wouldn't that make things worse for Nick? It was a big risk. Dared he take it?

Weariness overcame him before he found any answers.

CHAPTER ELEVEN

SIX weeks was a very long time.

After twelve years of separation from Freya, six weeks should have felt like a blink of an eye, but Gus had never been more impatient for the hours, days and weeks to fly.

Instead, time crawled with tedious, excruciating slowness.

Sure, the Arnhem Land project was still very interesting and important to him, but now there were two people who were so dear to his heart he hated the separation. Just the same, he'd already stolen weeks from the project and he needed to complete it before the wet season began, so he couldn't take more time off. As it was, he was working round the clock to have everything finished in time.

Nick was constantly on his mind. In a strange twist of fate, Gus now felt as if he was linked to his son more closely than most fathers could ever be. He delighted in every phone call and email as the boy continued on his road to full recovery.

As for Freya…

Gus spent far too much time thinking about Freya.

Number one in his thoughts was the amazing night they'd spent together. Over and over he replayed every precious moment. He would start with the dinner, recalling each shared glance across the table, each smile.

He'd remember how he and Freya had walked close beside the river, remember the longing, the electricity, the overpowering desire that consumed him. Then, later, the unreasoning joy of discovery—her longing matching his. Then the kisses, the caresses, the soft, sweet sighs of pleasure. The marvellous, passionate intimacy.

Their night had been so perfect, as sweet as when they were young, yet so much more powerful and poignant after the long, lonely journeys they'd both travelled.

There were other memories, too. So many wonderful memories of Freya, from the time he'd first seen her in Darwin till their damp-eyed farewell at Brisbane airport.

'I'll be back before Christmas,' he'd told her as he stole yet another last-minute kiss goodbye. 'And I'll make sure I'm back in plenty of time, so Nick won't have to worry.'

Despite the pressure of work, Gus was more determined than ever to keep his promise. He loved Nick. Loved Freya. Loved her with the deep, unavoidable, heart-grabbing certainty that had evaded him in his marriage.

He wasn't going to let her go a second time.

For most of November Freya was upbeat and optimistic. Nick was growing stronger every day and whenever Gus phoned or sent her an email, he was warm and affectionate and flirtatious and she was quite sure her most dearly cherished dreams were about to come true.

She just wished the time could pass more quickly. She wouldn't be completely at peace and happy until she saw Gus again and could look into his eyes and know she wasn't building up false hopes.

There were still black moments of doubt, especially when she lay in bed in the wee small hours and remembered that other time she'd been separated from Gus for six weeks and how much he'd changed in that time.

Could it happen again?

She told herself no. But she wished she could be absolutely sure. In reality, she was basing all her romantic hopes on the flimsiest of foundations— a few days in Brisbane when their emotions were running high and when nothing beyond the hospital had seemed real.

Had she been foolish to imagine that Gus cared for her deeply in the same way that she cared for him? If she really examined their recent relationship, there had only been a single evening of romance. One night of lovemaking between two consenting adults, who'd had a previous relationship, then turned to each other in a moment of huge emotional need.

Her past history with Gus hardly counted so, except for that one night, their shared love of Nick was their only point of connection. On that basis, could they really hope for a future together?

Their lifestyles were poles apart. Gus couldn't be expected to settle back into the quiet life of sleepy Sugar Bay, and he wouldn't want a woman and a boy trailing after him as he continued his important work in the world's remote outposts.

Although she knew all of this, Freya clung blindly to a vain hope. Those stolen moments with Gus had been so special. Memories of his electrifying touch, of his kisses, his voice, his smile…haunted her day and night.

She hadn't imagined the deeper meaning of those moments, had she?

If only she could be sure. If only it was Christmas already.

Gus scowled at the radar map on his computer screen. A huge low pressure system was moving across from the Indian Ocean and was about to dump its load on Australia's Top End.

Already, the sky was thick with cloud and the air was heavy and dense, making everyone's clothing stick to their skin. The smell of rain was in the air. It wouldn't be long before it arrived.

Damn.

The small plane destined to take him out of here wasn't due for another day, but once the rain arrived, the dirt airstrip here could be transformed in a matter of hours into a dangerously slippery mudslide. It would be impossible to land.

Gus had put through call after call, trying to locate a spare plane that could come sooner, but so far he'd had no luck.

He wondered if he should call Freya to warn her that he mightn't get away for Christmas after all.

Hell, no. He couldn't do that to her. Couldn't do it to Nick. He would find a way to get out of here, and there was no point in putting them through unnecessary worry.

Standing at the window, he watched the dark clouds roll in. If he started off now in the truck, he might reach the nearest all-weather airport in a day. He'd probably be racing against rising creek waters, but he'd get there.

He had to.

'I'm not wearing these stupid antlers. They're dumb as!' Nick sent the red velvet and pasteboard headpiece flying across the room.

'For heaven's sake,' Freya cried as she watched the antlers smash into the opposite wall. 'What's got into you, Nick? Pick them up right now.'

'Why should I?' Arms folded, Nick glowered at his mother. 'I don't need them. I'm not going to dumb old Carols by Candlelight. The songs are stupid and I hate Christmas.'

'I know you don't mean that.'

'I do.'

The boy was on the edge of tears, but he was fighting them valiantly and Freya's heart ached for him. It was such a disappointment to see him unhappy when he'd been doing so well. All the post-surgery worry and danger was behind Nick now and, apart from not being allowed to play football and the need for regular checks with their local GP, his life was miraculously back to normal. He'd been so looking forward to Christmas.

Damn Gus Wilder and his broken promises!

Freya wanted to throw something too—something that made a loud and satisfying smash. How could Gus do this to them after all his assurances?

Not that she could let Nick get away with such bad behaviour. Suppressing a sigh, she eyed her son. 'You asked me to buy those antlers and I paid good money for them, so the least you can do is pick them up.'

Her quiet, firm manner did the trick. Reluctantly, Nick collected the headpiece from the corner, but he showed no remorse as he fingered a broken antler prong.

'Bring it into the kitchen,' she said. 'I'll have to try to fix it with sticky tape.'

'What's the point of fixing it?'

She didn't bother to answer. She knew how fragile Nick's emotions were right now.

The timing for Gus's failure to show couldn't have been worse. The last few years, Nick always got tense the week before Christmas and, for him, Carols by Candlelight brought back the bitterest of memories. He'd been singing carols down on the beach with the Sugar Bay junior lifesavers on the night his grandfather had stolen away.

This year was going to be so much worse. Nick had been worked up for weeks and over the moon with excitement and anticipation because Gus was coming to the Bay. Gus had even named an arrival date a full week before Christmas.

Now they were four days past that date and there'd been no apology or explanation for Gus's no-show. Nick was devastated. Freya was furious.

And hurt.

And confused and disappointed.

With a heavy sigh, she looked across the room to their Christmas tree. She and Nick had scoured the seashore, searching for perfect branches of driftwood. They'd had so much fun and they'd come home, happy and excited, to arrange the silvery branches in a bucket of sand.

Then they'd hung tinsel and lights and Freya's delicate handmade ornaments alongside a variety of crude but cute Santas and angels that Nick had constructed over the years—a virtual record of every Christmas since he'd started kindergarten.

Beneath their tree, there now sat a red and green striped package with *'Dad'* written on the tag in Nick's clear handwriting. It was a book on the history of vampire legends for Gus. Nick was so proud of himself for tracking it down on the Internet.

And while Freya had tried to hide her excitement about Gus's return, she'd been as pumped as Nick, maybe more so. She'd been to the hairdresser's for glamorous streaks, and she'd had her legs waxed and her eyelashes tinted. She'd invested in new clothes in the hottest styles, including a slinky, summery dress and divinely sexy heels.

All to impress Gus Wilder.

But now she had to admit she'd been foolish.

She hadn't the heart to force Nick to go to the carols. The choir would manage without her boy. He could barely hold a tune anyway, not that it mattered. He sang with gusto and the night was all about community spirit rather than choral excellence.

'Well, this looks almost as good as new,' she said, holding up the mended antlers. 'But I suppose I'd better ring Maria and tell her you can't sing tonight. If we don't go to the carols, what would you like to do instead? We could go and see if the turtles have started making their nests.'

To her surprise, Nick didn't leap to accept her offer. Frowning glumly, he fiddled with the sticky tape dispenser. 'I s'pose I'd be letting the choir down if I stayed away.'

'Well…yes…I guess,' Freya echoed, surprised.

She waited, one curious eyebrow raised, but, as the seconds ticked on, her son didn't seem ready to explain his change of heart. 'We'd better get going then,' she said eventually. 'If you want to sing, you can't be late.'

Had she imagined it or had Nick's eyes betrayed a flash of excitement, even though he let out a theatrical sigh as he picked up the antlers and headed for the door?

Outside, a beautiful summer's twilight lingered and the beach was bathed in a soft mauve half-light. The sting had gone out of the day and a sweet breeze blew in from the ocean. Sugar Bay's families were making themselves comfortable on the grassy parkland at the edge of the sand, spreading picnic rugs and cushions.

Poppy was there, helping to hand out candles in cardboard holders. A stage was set at one end of the long lawn and children, wearing antlers and Santa caps, were lining up beside it.

'Off you go,' Freya told Nick and he dashed to join them, one hand holding the antlers in place as he ran.

Freya tossed a cushion onto the grass and flopped down onto it. She knew lots of people here, of course, and normally she'd be kept busy chatting and catching up on news, but tonight she wasn't in the mood to be social. She sat hugging her legs, with her chin propped on her knees, watching Nick in the distance as he joined the choir and exchanged shy greetings with a slim, very pretty girl with long dark hair.

Well, well, she thought. *Is Milla Matheson the reason Nick decided to come here after all?*

Her little boy was growing up.

She'd never felt more alone.

Damn you, Gus.

The light was fading swiftly. Glowing dots of candlelight appeared, dancing in the warm purple night like fireflies. Children ran on the grass waving coloured fluoro glow-sticks and their parents called to them to come and sit quietly, while the junior lifesavers' choir filed up make-shift steps and onto the stage.

Close by, the sea kept up its regular constant rhythm. Thump, dump, swish…

Everyone looked so happy, but behind Freya's eyelids hot tears gathered and her throat felt raw and painful. She was shaking, in danger of falling apart, and she knew she'd be a mess the minute the children started to sing. She always felt emotional when she saw them trying so hard to please their watching families. Tonight she was a dam about to burst.

She hugged her knees tighter and kept her eyes fixed on Nick in the back row of the choir, noticed that the mended antler prong was beginning to droop.

He looks so much like Gus, she thought with a pang, and then she swiftly cancelled that thought. *I'm so lucky he's well. I have no reason to be unhappy.*

But she had every reason to be angry.

Maria Carter, the choir's conductor, came onto the stage wearing a red and white polka dot sundress that showed off her tan. She tapped the microphone and smiled out at the crowd. Any minute now the singing would start. Freya hugged her knees more tightly than ever and kept her eyes on Nick.

Traditionally, he sent Freya a smile just before the singing started, but tonight his eyes were straying to the dark-haired girl in the row in front of him, and then out over the crowd.

Don't, Nick. Don't keep looking for Gus. You'll only break your heart. And mine.

Maria, the conductor, lifted her baton and Nick's face broke into a huge grin.

Concentrate, Nick.

The choir burst into an Aussie version of *Jingle Bells*, but Nick wasn't singing about dashing through the bush. He wasn't singing at all. He was grinning and waving to someone at the back of the crowd.

Freya stopped feeling weepy and began to feel embarrassed instead. Since when had her son developed behaviour problems? She turned around to see what had distracted him but it was so dark now, it was hard to see what had caught his attention.

And then her breathing snagged…

Poppy, clearly visible beneath a lamp post, was at the back of the crowd. There was no mistaking her silver hair and green kaftan. Beside her stood a tall, dark, manly figure…

Gus.

Freya's heart slammed against the wall of her chest.

Poppy was pointing in Freya's direction and Gus was listening carefully. He lifted a hand to shade his eyes from the lamp post's glare as he peered at the crowd, then he nodded. Next minute, he was moving, weaving his way through the crowd.

Freya tried to stand but her legs were like water. Her heart thudded madly as she watched the gleam of Gus's white shirt as he moved through the darkness and dancing candlelight.

No wonder Nick was smiling and forgetting to sing. Freya looked down at her old jeans and T-shirt and thought wistfully of her hot new outfits languishing at home.

This time when she tried to stand she was successful. She waved and Gus waved back, and she caught the white flash of his teeth as he smiled.

Stumbling over legs and apologising, she hurried to the edge of the crowd.

At last.

Gus hauled her into his arms and hugged her close and she felt the warmth and strength of him. She smelled his spicy cologne and his clean shirt, felt the thudding of his heartbeats, and she knew this was as good as it got.

Complete, perfect happiness.

Jingle Bells finished and the choir was given a round of hearty applause, and it was only then in the lull between carols, that Freya remembered she was supposed to be angry with Gus.

'Where have you been? You said you'd be here four days ago.'

'I know. I'm sorry.'

It was hard to be angry when Gus was fingering her hair and kissing her forehead.

'The wet season arrived early,' he said. 'The first of the big monsoons caught us all by surprise. The airstrip was too boggy for the plane to land so I had to drive to an all-weather strip, but the rivers and creeks were already flooding so there were more delays.' He looked down at her with a crooked smile. 'I fought flood waters and crocodiles to get here.'

Freya had to admit that, as excuses went, this was convincing. 'Couldn't you have let us know?'

Gus shook his head. 'All the lines were down and we had to rely on mobile phones, but a huge section of that Top End is out of the network. It was damn frustrating. I knew Nick would be disappointed.'

'Well, yes, he was. Very.'

'By the time I got to Darwin, my battery was

dead and I had to rush to make the plane, so I simply jumped on and hoped I'd surprise him.'

'He'll be thrilled,' Freya said, and she couldn't help smiling. Here they were, talking about Nick, who couldn't possibly be as thrilled as she was.

Gus held her closer. 'Nick looks well.'

'He is. He's never been better. All thanks to you.'

The choir began a new carol—*Deck the sheds with bits of wattle...*

Gus's arms encircled Freya, drawing her back against the solid wall of his chest. They stood like that, bodies aflame, at the edge of the crowd, watching and listening. Above them, stars appeared in the inky heavens and the warm December night seemed to close in around them—a benevolent and comforting darkness.

Freya might have felt completely at peace if she hadn't had so many questions and hopes and fears clashing in her head. Could she dare to assume that she was as important to Gus as Nick was?

As the second carol finished, Gus dipped his lips close to her ear. 'How long does this singing go on for?'

'Oh, about half an hour. Then Mel Crane dresses

up in a Father Christmas suit and drives in on a tractor, handing out ice creams to all the kids.' She turned in Gus's arms and searched his face. 'Why? Are you bored already?'

'Not bored.' His eyes sparkled and his lips brushed her ear. 'But I'm desperate to be alone with you.'

Freya's body zapped and flashed like a Christmas tree out of control. Perhaps it was just as well that another carol started—a song about six white kangaroos that pulled Santa's sleigh through the Outback.

She told herself not to get too excited. After all, it wasn't surprising that a bachelor, newly arrived from a remote outpost, might want to be alone with a woman. Just the same, her body continued to zap and flash, but somehow she remembered to keep breathing as one carol flowed into the next.

Then the children finished their last song and took their bows amidst a blaze of applause. Gus kept a tight hold on Freya's hand as they made their way to the front to greet Nick.

'Dad!' the boy yelled, practically leaping into Gus's arms.

A warm glow burned inside Freya as joyous grins spread over both Nick's and Gus's faces.

Gus told Nick how great the singing was and then he started to explain why he'd been delayed, but Nick didn't seem to care now that his dad was here. Gus's presence was all that mattered.

Pretty, dark-haired Milla Matheson walked past again and sent Nick an extra-bright smile. He waved to her, then stood on tiptoe and whispered something in Gus's ear.

Gus turned and took a surreptitious glance at the girl as she walked away, then he gave Nick a nod and a winking smile of approval.

'What are you two whispering about?' Freya *had* to ask.

Nick looked abashed and Gus laughed. 'Secret men's business.' Then he looped one arm around the boy's shoulders while he drew Freya to him. 'Nick was just pointing out a nice sensible girl from his class at school.'

'Oh.' It was the only response Freya could manage. When she was this close to Gus, her brain went into meltdown and she could think of nothing but him, of how she felt about him, how she wished…

Oh, dear God, was she wishing for too much?

She was feeling shaky again as Poppy made her way towards them.

'You sang like angels!' she exclaimed, giving her grandson a bear hug that knocked his antlers sideways. Poppy beamed at Freya and Gus. 'Weren't the children wonderful?'

'Wonderful,' they agreed.

'And now the ice creams are on their way.' Poppy sent Gus a pointed glance.

'Yes.' Gus took Freya's hand. 'And it seems to me that if Nick's going to be guzzling ice cream, this is the perfect time for me to take his mother for a walk.'

'Can't I come, too?' asked Nick.

'I thought you were lining up for ice cream?'

The boy shrugged.

'Thing is, I have something very important to say to your mum,' Gus said, making Freya's heart leap. 'But I promise we won't be too long.'

'Take as long as you like,' Poppy told them. 'Nick and I won't mind waiting. Will we, Nick?'

The boy looked as if he might disagree, but

something in Poppy's expression must have changed his mind.

'Sure.' Nick's face was split by a sudden grin. 'We don't mind how long you take.'

'You know, those two are jumping to all sorts of conclusions,' Freya told Gus as he led her away from the crowds and onto the dark, deserted beach.

His response was a long look deep into her eyes and a smile that made her face flame.

Hastily, she tried to think of something else to say. 'Um…if we're going to walk on the sand, we should probably take off our shoes.'

'Good idea.'

They left their shoes beside a pile of rocks, then walked towards the water. The sea was relatively flat with only small waves lapping the shore, and the tide was out, leaving an expanse of firm sand that was cool and damp beneath their bare feet. On the horizon, a beautiful almost full moon was rising.

Freya took deep breaths of clean sea air, hoping it might help her to calm down.

Gus's arm was around her shoulders again. 'It's

so good to be back,' he said. 'It's so beautiful here, so quiet. I always feel at peace.'

'That's why the Bay's such a popular holiday destination.'

Gus stopped in his tracks.

Freya's heart took a dive. 'What's the matter?'

'I was talking rubbish. It's not this *place* that gives me peace. I've been to oodles of quiet and beautiful places but I've never felt how I feel when I'm with you, Freya.' He took both her hands in his. 'In Brisbane, with all the medical drama on the go, whenever I was with you, I felt—'

'Peaceful?'

In the moonlight she saw Gus's smile.

'Not peaceful exactly. Most of the time I was filled with blinding lust—but I was happy. Bone-deep happy. Like I'd been sailing for a long time, lost at sea, and I'd found a perfect mooring.'

He trapped her hands against his chest and held them there, enclosed in his hands.

She could feel his heartbeats.

His throat rippled. 'I was hoping…that maybe… you might feel—'

'I do,' Freya whispered. 'I'm exceptionally happy whenever I'm with you.'

'Floss.' Her old nickname floated on the night air as he pulled her in and kissed her.

It was a long time before they walked on, arms about each other, skirting the edge of the water, and Freya was no longer worried. She was drenched in happiness.

'We were always meant for each other,' Gus said. 'You know that, don't you?'

'But I made the worst mistake when I didn't tell you about the baby.'

'I was as much to blame. I was a conceited uni brat and I never gave you a proper chance to explain. But that's behind us. Now we have the future.'

'Are you saying—?'

'Yes.' Gus's finger traced the shape of Freya's ear. 'I'm saying that I love you, Floss. I've been thinking about little else for the past six weeks. I was so anxious to get here to ask you to marry me.'

Marry.

Freya stumbled. She couldn't help it. Her knees gave way completely and she sank towards the sand.

Taken by surprise, Gus tried to catch her, but

when she grabbed at his shirt she tipped him off balance.

Next moment they landed in a tangled heap.

Splash.

A wave washed over them.

'Are you all right?' Gus sounded worried.

'I'm fine.' Freya was laughing, helpless with surprise.

Sandy and damp, they clung together, breaking into giggles like teenagers.

'Sorry about that,' Freya gasped between giggles.

Another wave washed in, soaking them again and they didn't care. They rolled closer and lay in their wet clothes, grinning goofily and gazing at the glistening stars in each other's eyes.

'I didn't mean to shock you.' Gus lifted a damp strand of hair from her face.

'It's OK. Being proposed to is the best kind of shock.'

'But you didn't give me an answer.'

'Didn't I?' Freya kissed him, adoring the cool saltiness on his lips. 'I meant to say yes. I'd love to marry you, Gus Wilder.'

Another long and lovely kiss and another

soaking wave later, Freya said, 'But how's it going to work? Do you have any plans for us?'

Gus's happy gaze searched her face. 'Does it matter? At the moment, all I want is for you and me and Nick to be together. I don't really mind where we are or what happens, as long as we're a family.'

'Sounds good to me. I'd be happy to go anywhere if you were there, and as long as Nick had access to decent health care.'

'We'd make sure of that.' He drew her into him. 'Mmm,' he whispered, trailing kisses over her throat. 'I've always thought of you as my sexy mermaid.'

Suddenly, the kisses stopped as Gus sat up. 'Hell.' Swearing softly, he patted at his damp pockets.

'What's the matter?' Freya sat up too. 'Have you lost something?'

'I hope not.'

Gus's face was grim and distinctly worried as he dealt with a button on his shirt pocket. Of course, the task would have been so much easier if his clothes weren't wringing wet.

At last, he had the pocket open and he reached

inside. 'Thank God. I thought it might have washed out.'

'What is it? Your wallet? Your phone?'

'This,' Gus said, reaching for her hand, and he slipped a ring onto her finger.

'Ohhhh.' Freya saw the flash of silver and diamonds and the gleam of a dark faceted stone and she gasped at the enormity of what might have happened if the ring had been lost. 'An engagement ring,' she whispered.

'You can't see it properly in this light, but the main stone's a sapphire. A mixture of blue and green to match your eyes.'

'Gus, I love it. I'd love it if it was made of barbed wire, but this is gorgeous.'

'What happened to you two?' Poppy tut-tutted as Gus and Freya finally arrived back from the beach with sodden clothes and dripping hair. 'You look like a pair of good-for-nothing teenagers.'

'I almost drowned trying to ask Freya to marry me,' Gus said, grinning happily.

This was met by squeals from Poppy and Nick.

'And then we got engaged but we were more

or less underwater,' Freya added, laughing as she held out her hand to show them her beautiful ring.

This news was greeted by even more satisfying reactions. Nick gave another squealing whoop and broke into a war dance. Poppy smiled enormously and hugged them both, wet clothes and all.

It was a week later, with the happiest Christmas ever behind them, that Gus told Freya about his parents' surprise.

They were walking along the beach as they did most afternoons, floating on happiness, still marvelling that being together could be so good, that life could feel so wonderful. Nick was there too, running ahead of them with Urchin, throwing a ball for the dog to catch.

'See this land,' Gus said, pointing to a vacant double allotment that fronted both the beach and the mouth of a small creek.

'It's fabulous, isn't it?' Freya said. 'The best piece of untouched real estate in the Bay.'

'My father bought it when he was living here.

I guess, being a bank manager, he had an eye for a good investment.'

Freya's lovely eyes widened. 'I hope he hung on to it. It must be worth a fortune now.'

'He hung on to it,' Gus said quietly, then he smiled. 'He and Mum want to give the land to us as a wedding present.'

Her shock must have rendered her speechless. It was ages before she spoke. 'That's so generous,' she said at last. 'But—' She frowned and looked out to sea, to the dancing waves and dazzling sun pennies. 'But would you want to build a home here? Wouldn't it be too much of a tie?'

Gus chuckled, felt the excitement inside him begin to bubble over. 'Ever since Dad's phone call on Christmas Day, I've been hatching a plan. I'd like to build a cluster of cottages here for the families of seriously ill children. It would be somewhere peaceful, with a holiday atmosphere for them to come to—after a big operation perhaps, or chemotherapy. A place for the whole family to relax and recover.'

Freya was shaking her head.

'You don't like the idea?'

'I do like it,' she said. 'I'm just taking it in.'

'It's what I do best, Freya. I've got the experience and the contacts.'

'And we both know what it's like to have a seriously ill child.'

'So I'd have your support?'

Her eyes were shining. 'Absolutely.'

'We could stay on here then,' Gus said. 'At least until Nick finishes school. You could run your gallery. I'd set up a foundation to fund the cottages, and manage the construction. I'd create a website to handle publicity and bookings.'

'It sounds perfect.' Freya was laughing and hugging him. 'Gus, I can't imagine anything better.'

'I can,' he said, gathering her into him.

'What's that?' she asked on a breathless whisper as he began to kiss her bare shoulder.

'A lifetime with you.'

As he kissed her again, he heard a boy's happy shout and a dog's bark and the slap and roll of the sea.